Noble
Stories

Marc Ridge

Forwarded and edited by
Chad Chisholm

Twin Takes Press

An imprint of New Watermill House

Published by Twin Takes Press

Clinton, Mississippi

ISBN: 978-0-578-83748-2

ACKNOWLEDGMENTS

The editor thanks Paul Schleifer for proofreading these pages and providing feedback on the stories. Paul and Marc never met, but they would have been friends. The editor also thanks Margaret Delashmit, to whom Marc's family donated his literary estate—many thanks to Margaret for her support and inspiration. The editor also expresses appreciation for Marc's family and members of the Rust College faculty who wanted these stories to be published. Finally, the editor expresses his appreciation to Greg Sellers for his advice on the title (which might have been the work of a moment for him, but was a godsend in the 'nick of time' for me). Versions of these stories appeared in *Mallorn* and *Freedom's Hill Primer* and are reprinted here courtesy of The Tolkien Society and the Carolina Institute for Faith and Culture. Previously published stories might appear altered or changed, and there are two main reasons for this: (1) changes made by the author who sometimes revised even after his tales were printed; (2) efforts by the editor to provide continuity between chapters to enable the reader to transition with more ease between stories. The cover image is courtesy of Pixabay. The authorial picture is courtesy of *The Daily Journal* (Franklin, Indiana).

TABLE OF CONTENTS

DEDICATION

For students and colleagues throughout the years—

Nihil est melius quam vita diligentissima.

"...Men's lives are short.
The hard man and his cruelties will be
cursed behind his back, and mocked in death.
But one whose heart and ways are kind—of him
strangers will bear report to the wide world,
and distant men will praise him."
—*The Odyssey* (Book XIX)
  Robert Fitzgerald, translator

FORWARD

MANY COLLABORATIONS

MARC RIDGE, ever since I met him, had wanted to write an episodic novel (though he never called it that) about a group of young people in rural Indiana: each of these stories was an enduring preoccupation for him.

I cannot be exact about when Professor Ridge developed these Noble tales, but I believe most of them were written between 2008 and 2010, when I left our college campus to complete doctoral coursework in the Dallas-Fort Worth area. A few stories were composed perhaps two or three years after I returned from Texas, but I believe many of them existed in drafts before I returned.

Though I remember Ridge discussing themes and personalities and settings, he shared no drafts with me until autumn 2010 or spring 2011. Versions of these stories were later workshopped in my home, and some (such as "Lloyd" and "Werewolf Hollow") were printed in literary journals, though I can verify their existence years before their publication.

That said, the archetypes of these tales preexisted the compositions now before us.

***

I first encountered Professor Ridge at a faculty meeting in August 2005. If memory continues to serve, he bluntly if not unkindly asked me, "Are you another of these dreary academics?" Despite what others might view as an inauspicious introduction, we were shortly afterwards meeting in offices and rooms to discuss literature, mythology, philosophy, metaphysics, religion, film, popular culture, history, and, almost always, storytelling. The two of us were neighbors who lived in faculty housing, so we often discussed such topics until about 3am—the time Ray Bradbury called *the soul's midnight.*

Our friendship led to many collaborations. Professor Ridge and I worked on projects for our English Department and his writing center—these ventures ranged from revising the proficiency exam rubric to editing student content for a campus newsletter. However, our principal passions were for imaginative narrative and other worlds: whether discussing Arthurian legends or science fiction, Latin-based etymologies or binary notations, this passion formed the foundation of our fellowship. This is what beckoned us evening after evening, weekend after weekend, to seek the kindred comfort and sustenance that we found in one another.

During our gatherings, Professor Ridge shared with me fragments of his created world. Our venues varied. Sometimes I recall the mixed aroma of hot pepperonis and beer fizz at the local pizzeria; other times, I remember the plain but pleasant scents of black tea and toasted sandwiches in our faculty apartments; usually there were various books of text or illustrations about, along with a chessboard or playing cards scattered about the table.

During such times, often with an album of medieval choral music or midcentury American jazz playing in the background, Professor Ridge discussed how his characters as children began to encounter supernatural forces, and that these occurrences would grow as his characters became teenagers and adults. As I write this, I see him reclining on a red sofa—an article of furniture that my wife and I were recently (and regrettably) persuaded to part with—as he muses about Michael Bear having a gift for courage and love, but who would also suffer terribly; he often spoke of Caitlyn and Caryn (whom he sometimes referred to as Sabon and Annetta) as Maud Gonne figures for the narrator and Michael.

On those late nights, I remember Marc Ridge looking towards but not really seeing the ceiling fan, and I believe he inwardly transformed into the characters he described: the traumatic events shared by Michael, Jase, Caryn, Jenna, Tippy, and the narrator would stretch his face and change his voice as he described the preternatural forces that aided or aligned against them, and I felt him moved to his deepest soul while conveying the despair and redemption that each of them had to undergo. When it comes to these characters, I believe Professor Ridge lent part of his life to them: they lived, quite deeply, through him, and thus, at times, seemed to take on figurative flesh.

These remembrances illustrate how *Noble Stories* was developing in the mind of the maker decades before their publication, and I believe these characters haunted Professor Ridge long before he had stories fitted for them.

These fictional souls, after being carried so long by their creator, are now ours. May we learn and delight in them.

INTRODUCTION

Summer 1997

BIRDSONG RINGING through the forest in predawn turmoil of summer awakens me. The sharply sweet aroma of pine trees fills my nostrils with energy, bringing me to full consciousness. Walking barefoot from the loft down the white pine staircase and into the kitchen, I flip on the coffee pot; as it sputters to life dripping the dark liquid into a carafe stained brown, I begin cooking the same breakfast I've eaten throughout much of my adult life—scrambled eggs with onion and green peppers, cubed hash browns and sausage links soaked in beer.

I take breakfast and coffee onto the porch of my cabin to watch the sun rising over Kentucky Lake. The hand-carved antique rocker, that once belonged to Tava—Michael's grandmother—squeaks on the aged boards of the porch as if crying out for a return to the carefree days of youth. That is ironic since the 1960s and early 70s were anything but carefree.

As I eat, feeling the white-yellow rays of the sun stretching out to warm the soul, I think about Michael and Jase, and the women we knew and loved, and those long rides on horseback—all lost now in shadow. Gone now are the horses, the women, and Jase; I do not know if Michael is alive because I have not heard from him since Jase's funeral a couple of years back. All I have left of those crazy days during the decade of love is Michael's 1969 metallic green GTX. Even after thirty years, the sweet aroma of roses and violets still fills the interior of the car. Sometimes, when I am driving alone down the country roads at night, I can sense the gang in the car with me: Jenna telling me to go slower; Jase urging me to go faster; Tippy, eyes wide-open; Michael and Caryn sitting together in the front seat eyeing me with concern.

Every few days I walk two miles down a fire trail into the small hamlet. I buy groceries at a little rustic store operated by an old couple who seem happy to live uncomplicated lives in hill-town America. On June 21st, I enter the store and see someone familiar, yet different, standing behind the counter. An ageless comely woman with bushy brown hair smiles up at me from an article she is reading in *Time* magazine, and winks.

"Hello. We have a special on our home-cooked dinner today. Meatloaf and buttery mashed potatoes with sliced green beans covered in baby onions. You interested?"

I take the carryout container after gathering up some other supplies and thank her. I usually don't buy meals there, but this time is different. As I look into her eyes that seem to sparkle between blue, green, azure, and brown, I see images of all the women I have known, loved, and lost.

I blink.

"Oh, and there's a telegram for you." Her sweet voice is hypnotic.

"What?" How does she even know who I am? I think quickly.

"Well, there's no addressee, but since you are the only writer around these parts, I figure it is for you."

It is a small town. Even newcomers hear stories. The owners must have described me to her. These and other thoughts quickly race through my mind and are quickly forgotten.

I take the dog-eared telegram. The words *To The Writer, From Michael* are written neatly on the outside. As I am about to leave, the woman says, "Only the Moirai know their meaning. Life is to be experienced, not questioned."

I begin to say something, but the woman smiles and turns her attention back to the article. When I arrive back at the cabin, I open the telegram. It has just one line written in Michael's nervous handwriting: 'I need to see you NOW about something important!'

I sit heavily on the sofa with a sigh. After not hearing a peep from Michael since Jase's funeral in 1995, he sends me this message. My gaze travels slowly through the open door at the encroaching darkness, and I shiver involuntarily.

My summer was going to suddenly get interesting.

I fall asleep on the sofa and images from the past flicker through my dreams...

FIRST PHASE

THEY WERE YOUNG

CHAPTER ONE

LLOYD

DURING THE AUTUMN of 1963 I learned the real difference between being rich and being poor. I had always thought that my family was poor. Dad said we were beggars, but Mom said we were middle-class poor. Both my parents seemed to earn enough money, but for some reason they always ran short of cash towards the end of the month. Don't get me wrong, we never went hungry–unlike my closest friend's family did nearly every week.

Jason Hoag's father was the town drunk in Noble, Indiana, during the sixties, leaving Jase's mother precious little money for groceries. Many days, all Jase had to eat would be a cheese sandwich and that warmed-over compartment food the school called 'lunch.' Even though Mom worked a full-time job, she saw to it that I ate two hot meals at home (breakfast and supper) and fixed us (my brother, sister and me) bag lunches consisting of fried egg sandwiches or BLTs—or, to my horror, chicken or tuna salad—an apple or orange and a Ding Dong or two. And, of course, every morning she left me some money for snacks and mid-afternoon milk.

During most of his life, Dad worked as a truck driver. He earned decent money, but most of it went to such expenses as insurance, state, county and federal taxes, and monthly payments for the purchase of the truck. Such were the pleasures, and curses, of being one's own boss.

Mom worked for Sears when it was still 'Sears & Roebuck.' She was assistant head cashier—not the kind that stands at the cash register with dull glazed looks and judging you for purchasing, with plastic cards, merchandise you probably can't afford anyway; she was an integral part of handling the records and money for the entire store. Hours were reasonable and pay satisfactory, although not overly exciting.

Their paychecks combined were able to pay for a new house, furniture, and two cars, not to mention the care and feeding of four horses. Every August my older brother, sister, and I were forced to accompany Mom to Sears & Roebuck for the purchasing of new school clothes (with mild complaints from Mom that we needed to learn to stop growing so fast). Moreover, holidays at my house seemed like a Norman Rockwell painting with decorations everywhere, the aroma of assorted foods—hams, turkey, potatoes, sweet potatoes and such—cooking in the kitchen, intermingled with the sweet smell of chocolate and peanut butter fudge, and freshly heated apple cider.

Even so, I still thought of us as poor.

Jase and I had another friend we were sure was rich; however, he never lorded his position over us or even let on that he noticed our financial situations were much different from his. He was fond of saying things like, 'it'll all even out someday,' and, 'it's only money.' Of course, back in 1963, about the only things we really cared about were drinking sodas and going to the movies, so we didn't really need much money anyway. (Soda costing about a dime for a twelve-ounce bottle and a day at The Themis theater right around thirty-five cents for two shows.)

Our friend, Michael J. Bear of the Indiana Bears, was not exactly Old World money, but he was still better off than most because he received a weekly allowance of twenty dollars; it was given to him by his father for, as he'd say, 'just being a good kid.'

Jase and I had to work our rears off cleaning horse stalls and mowing lawns (five dollars per lawn and three dollars per stall), which was in addition to all the other work we were expected to do out to the Noble Horse Barns. And, of course, Jase would often give much of his money to his mother to help buy food for the family.

Michael refused payment when he'd help us, saying that being allowed to do the work was reward enough.

Noble, Indiana, is a small town of only about ten-odd thousand residents, many of whom live on the outlying farms. It has two elementary schools, so no one living in town has to walk further than a mile one way to school, which is handy during the winter months when snow can get as high as three feet. Economically, there isn't really much difference between the greater portion of residents. Many of the more affluent people live on the South Side of town in older but more expensive houses. The moderate-income families live predominately on the East and North Sides in newer prefab houses on neatly designed lots in neighborhoods known for their prosperity according to the design of the houses available for the lots. Designs in 1963 consisted mainly of one-story two and three bedroom homes without garages to two-story four and five bedroom homes with attached two car garages on a full half acre of land.

In-between the Upper North Side and the Lower East Side are the two-story duplexes. These low rent neighborhoods comprise what my friends and I dubbed the Noble Slums. A place my family lived until my Mom decided she'd had enough of paying rent for substandard housing, and bought one of those cracker-box prefab houses on the East Side in 1961. During our school years, Jase's family never was able to escape the duplexes.

Jase, Michael and I have been friends since kindergarten— somehow managing to even be placed in the same classrooms throughout elementary school. In sixth grade, a new kid came to our school, a boy named Lloyd Johnson.

Lloyd was small for his age and spent all of his free time with his head on his desk sleeping or crying. Well, not all of his free time was spent like that. Sometimes he'd just stare off into space. It was something that gave the girls in the class the creeps. Mainly because you'd think he was looking at you with those dull-witted filmy eyes, when in fact he was hardly aware of anything going on around him. It seemed to me at the time that our teacher, Mrs. Krule, took pleasure in slamming her yardstick on Lloyd's desk.

"Lloyd! Wake up!" She did this about seven times a day although it never did any good. Lloyd seemed lost in a world far removed from the one that confined the rest of us.

If my family was middle-class poor and Jase's family was real poor, then Lloyd's had to be dirt poor. I could tell Lloyd didn't really care much about what the other kids thought of him, or the fact that he was less better off than they were. The dull, faraway look on his tired face proved he just figured that was how things were meant to be. Much of the teasing centered upon Lloyd's hygiene practices, or lack thereof. Whenever the other kids would tease Lloyd, Jase would step in to defend him, which meant I'd end up having to pull Jase off some smart-lipped kid before knives came out and real damage occurred.

As far as I knew, Lloyd owned two pairs of pants and perhaps three shirts, all of which, judging from their condition, he probably owned since fourth grade. His skin always had a grayish coloring to it, almost like someone had rubbed ash into his flesh until no amount of scrubbing could make the dirt disappear. During the time I knew him, the dark circles around his eyes began to grow worse earning him the nickname of Spooky—a name Jase, Michael and I loathed and never used in reference to Lloyd. Even though I came to know that Lloyd did wash thoroughly every day, for all the good it did him, he still produced a strange odor that was mildly offensive by lunchtime. But a lot of kids had odors during the first stages of puberty; especially, one girl in our class who truly stank and was often teased by our classmates as being 'Lloyd's wife.'

Yes, Jenna stank. Really stank. I sat in the back of the first row, and she sat in the back of the sixth row, mercifully near an open window, and I still choked from her smell if a strong breeze sprang up. Everyone in the class thought she stank because she didn't bathe, but around the middle of September we discovered the truth—a truth that got me thinking more about hygiene. Of course, I didn't have a problem except from Mom's point of view. She was always commenting on my habit of taking three showers a day and washing my hair every morning, saying that every other day would be enough.

It happened one Friday after lunch. The school nurse came to our classroom, spoke conspiratorially with our teacher—each of them casting glances now and then towards Jenna. Ten minutes passed before the nurse left and Mrs. Krule addressed the class.

"Jenna, come up here please."

Our attention was riveted on what was going to happen to Jenna and nobody said a word. Lloyd, of course, already had his head down and was fast asleep. As Jenna walked to the front of the class, I heard some boy mutter something about a G.I. bath. I knew what that was because Dad had told me stories about what soldiers did to their comrades who didn't bathe regularly. (The platoon would get together, strip the offender down, and scrub him with steel wool and lye soap. I had a fleeting vision of the nurse in her office preparing such an experience for Jenna.)

"Jenna, take this note home to your mother and father, and tell them to call me right away." Jenna took the note with her eyes on the floor.

"Yes, Missus Krule."

"And you're excused from school until you can bring me a doctor's note saying you're clean."

Michael poked me in the arm to get my attention and said, "Lice, man. Jenna has cooties."

I looked over at the sleeping Lloyd and wondered if cooties could make someone's skin turn gray and make them sleep all the time.

After Jenna went home, Mrs. Krule talked to us about lice and that they had nothing to do with whether or not someone bathed on a regular basis. She also explained to us how Jenna's parents were poor farmers and that she could only take one hot bath a week because they used well water and were having problems at the moment, which is why she developed such an odor by mid-week. Until that day I took for granted that everyone had unlimited access to hot, running water, and began to feel a little guilty that my parents were able to give me so much. After that day, I cut back to only two showers a day.

It took my friends and me most of September to warm up to Lloyd, mostly because he'd keep to himself on the playground and disappear shortly after school. Even so, we took notice of how little Lloyd had to eat for lunch and wondered if he ever ate dinner. None of the other kids would sit near Lloyd during lunch. The boys just didn't like him and the girls said his smell ruined their appetites. Michael said Lloyd may be puny but that wasn't any reason to make him an outcast. Besides, he said, Lloyd didn't smell any worse than Jase on an average day. So one day, Michael, Jase and I sat with Lloyd just to spite the other kids.

Our move surprised Lloyd enough that he sort of began speaking to us. I say it this way because our first conversation with Lloyd consisted of squished-up eyes, a nod here and there, and several grunts we took to mean 'yes' or 'no' depending on the tone and duration.

"Lloyd, mind if we join you?" This from Michael, our self-appointed leader. There was a look of surprise on Lloyd's face.

"Hey, man, I seem to have an extra milk. You want it?" Jase remarked trying to act cool. Lloyd raised his eyebrows and wiped his lips with his tongue.

"Ugh. Tuna salad sandwiches again. Hey, Lloyd, you want part of this…I'm kinda tuna'd out this week," I remarked as I noticed that for the fifth day in a row Mom had fixed me two tuna salad sandwiches.

Swoop, grasp, and short grunt from Lloyd as he grabbed and devoured the tuna sandwich I handed to him.

Lloyd never thanked us afterwards, so I figured it wasn't a word he'd learned as of yet. Michael said it might take a while before Lloyd could store up enough energy to allow him to speak. Jase just stared with a faraway look on his face at Lloyd as he ate. I guess that having gone to bed with an empty stomach on more than one occasion made Jase feel a sort of kinship with Lloyd that Michael and I didn't then understand.

During the afternoon recess while we played a game of kickball, I nailed the ball into the parking lot and saw Lloyd go after it. He brought it back and asked if he could be on my team. I looked down at his tattered sneakers with only half-laces and said, "Sure, but if your shoe comes off while you're running bases don't stop to pick it up. Just keep running."

During the following two weeks, sharing our lunches with Lloyd became a ritual. Slowly, Lloyd began to open up to us and even seemed to be sleeping less in class after lunch. Our actions didn't go unnoticed by Mrs. Krule, who one day brought over a tray of hot food to our table for Lloyd.

"Young men need a hot meal now and then, Lloyd."

I saw a tear well up in Lloyd's eye when Mrs. Krule added, "Tell your mother to come to school tomorrow. I want to speak with her."

Then she smiled at my friends and me, and without speaking let us know how proud she was of us.

Halloween weekend we invited Lloyd to join us for a sleepover at Michael's house. Michael's parents were going to be away the entire weekend, and Jase and I often stayed with him at such times. We thought the experience would be good for Lloyd. Besides, Sammy Terri was having a 'monsterthon' on Channel 4 Friday night, and it seemed like a good lead-in for the weekend of mischief.

But first we had one hurdle to clear—Lloyd's mother.

We'd heard stories about Lloyd's mom from some of the small-time cowboys at the horse barns. Words like 'whore,' 'slut,' and 'pass-around-lay' brought strange and intriguing images to our prepubescent minds. She was the type of woman who seemed to breed rumors as easily and often as she bred children. (Something of an irony since Lloyd was her only child.) One story, we learned for a fact to be true, centered on the young age at which she'd had Lloyd: a stigma that haunted her into semi-isolation in our town.

She worked the nightshift at the Steer restaurant out on Highway 37 near the edge of town and rarely went out shopping during the day, which is one reason none of us had ever seen her. Another reason was that Lloyd never invited us to his home for play or sleepovers. And he never spoke about her during the few times we'd gotten him to hangout with us after school. So, it was a major event when we, in a group, went to Lloyd's home to ask his mother's permission for him to spend Halloween weekend with us at Michael's house.

Lloyd lived with his mom in a rundown hotel, in what we laughingly referred to as 'downtown.' In some ways, Noble was like Rome, in that all roads led to downtown. Like most small towns, the town square was comprised of the county courthouse and several stores. Among the businesses on the square were Montgomery's Department Store, Noble Hardware—owned and operated by Gene Noble whose great grandparents had helped found the town way back during the Civil War—and a smattering of small Mom & Pop stores that sold everything from general auto parts to candy and soda fountain drinks.

Just one block off the square, next to The Themis, was the Blake Hotel where Lloyd and his mother lived.

I accompanied Michael and Jase to Lloyd's home on a Friday after school, Lloyd reluctantly following behind with head bowed. Something seemed to be weighing more heavily on Lloyd's mind that day than was usual, so my friends and I kept silent knowing that Lloyd would let us into his thoughts when he was ready. However, we all suspected what was troubling Lloyd—he was ashamed of where he lived. Of course, none of us realized how poor Lloyd and his mother truly were.

The march through autumn leaves from Robin Hood Elementary to downtown was somber. We looked like a mini-parade of economic representations of the various social strata that made up our small town.

Michael was in the lead wearing expensive penny loafers, designer slacks and dress shirt, and leather jacket imported from Italy; myself, dressed in my Sears & Roebuck Levi jeans, turtleneck shirt and cotton sweater, and new Converse All Stars sneakers; Jase in his faded plaid pants, blue cabana shirt from the local thrift store, a hand-me-down jean jacket used by both his older brother and sister, and worn-out cowboy boots; followed by Lloyd in a faded and stained button-up shirt, faded jeans showing the white threads of wear, and worn out sneakers with broken laces and holes in the soles, wrapped in a jacket best suited for the rag pile than being used as protection from the brisk October weather.

As we approached the hotel, we saw some of the local 'cools' sitting on the stoop smoking cigarettes and drinking early beers. None of whom paid us any mind as we filed silently past them up the stairs and through the wooden doors into the main atrium.

Though amazed at the dilapidated condition of the lobby, I could see the hotel had been a misplaced jewel for such a backwater town. The floor was covered in a ragged and frayed carpet that at one time must have been considered a true treasure. Upon it was a colorful design of the state flag and capitol building in Indianapolis—bright blues and gold and silver stitching—that had become dull with age and worn grooves where an army of feet had tramped across its surface. A cobwebbed crystal chandelier made of gold-plating and dulled silver, hung from the tall ceiling, its five remaining bulbs casting a dull almost yellow light upon the floor and check-in desk where a bald man in his sixties leaned unconcerned upon the dark wood counter reading a copy of the local newspaper. He glanced up once, squinting at us, then waved sadly at Lloyd as we turned to ascend the staircase. After sneezing twice because of the musty dustiness of the place, I followed my friends up three flights of stairs, stepping over refuse, forgotten toys, and at least one dead rat. The squeaky wooden stairs seemed to moan in pain as we ascended, holding on to the rickety banister that threatened to collapse if held too tightly.

The apartment where Lloyd and his mother lived was nothing more than a ten-foot square room with attached kitchenette and a small bedroom. In the living room was a dusty brown little sofa. I saw an old pillow and sheet, neatly folded, lying on one end with a ratty blanket, and figured that must be Lloyd's bed. The only other pieces of furniture in the room were an old coffee table and a black & white television sitting forlornly on a crate.

As we crowded into the apartment, Lloyd's mother came out of the bedroom dressed in a tattered night coat, her long blond hair mussed and tangled.

"Hello, boys."

Her soft voice sounded like gravel and dust. I was stunned to see a round milky breast pop out of her gown as she shambled to the sofa and plopped down. In her left hand was a brown envelope; her right fist clutched around the long neck of a bottle of Tennessee whisky. She took a long drink before letting the bottle slip to the floor where the liquid pooled around her feet. Falling back into the cushions she motioned Lloyd over.

"Come here, sweetie."

Lloyd tilted the bottle upright before kneeling next to his mother, and gently closed her gown. She smiled wanly, ran her thin fingers through his hair, and began to cry.

"Mom?" Lloyd began crying, and looked to us for help. Not really knowing what else to do, we gathered around him offering what support we could.

"Go in the bedroom and get your suitcase. I've already packed it," whispered his mother in a tired gravelly voice.

A heavy rapping on the door we'd left open made us turn in surprise. In the doorway stood a short stern-looking woman with long brown hair in a business outfit holding a clipboard and brown briefcase. Robert Brown, the County Sheriff, stood stoically next to her.

"Miss Johnson?" The stern-looking woman spoke in a commanding, yet gentle, voice. "Hi. My name's Cloe Goodheart, from Child Care Services. I presume you received my letter?"

Lloyd's mother lowered her eyes and nodded.

"He'll just be a minute. I haven't told him yet."

"You boys should probably wait outside," said the sheriff who ushered us out of the apartment.

Outside, Jase sat on the stoop, his eyes locked on the sheriff's patrol car. I knew he was thinking about his father who was most probably sitting at Poole's Bar a couple of blocks away talking shop with the happy hour crowd, working on his own weekend bender. Michael walked down the street, hands in pockets. What he was thinking I could not even guess. I stood alone near the curb, my eyes moving from my friends to the semi-cools.

One of the cools drew a cigarette from the pack with his teeth, rolled the pack into the sleeve of his t-shirt and lit a match. As I watched the tip of the cigarette burn red, gray smoke curling up around his face, two high school girls in poodle skirts strolled past. The cools whistled appreciatively; the girls giggled and flipped their hair, their hips swaying with inviting suggestiveness. I watched the girls disappear around the corner where Michael was standing. One of the Cools made a joke I didn't hear. A car with two older women, I guessed them to be from the local college, stopped and the Cools got in. As the car sped off, the stern woman came out of the hotel with Lloyd in tow.

He was crying, but didn't appear to be putting up a fight. Settling Lloyd into the backseat of her car, the woman glanced at me, winked, smiled sadly, and drove away. A minute later, the sheriff came out with Lloyd's mother. She was dressed, and I saw that she'd been handcuffed. After putting her into the back of his patrol car, the sheriff placed a strong hand on my shoulder.

"You and your friends should probably go on home now. Have your father call me later."

"Yes sir," I said, a little confused and feeling more than a little empty inside.

Michael came up to Jase and me, sighed heavily, and said, "Well, guys, guess I'll see ya later."

"Yeah," Jase and I said in unison.

We learned later, from the wanna-be-cowboys out at the horse barns, that Lloyd's mother had been arrested for prostitution and child neglect, and had been sent to the state prison for a year. Lloyd just disappeared. My parents told me that he'd been sent to the Home for Boys up in Indianapolis.

During dinner the night Lloyd was taken away, I sat in silence with my brother, sister, mother and father, staring at the meatloaf and mashed potatoes on my plate, as my mother said grace. After she said 'amen,' I added silently, "Please watch over Lloyd and his mother."

NOTE

Published in Freedom's Hill Primer *on September 27, 2017. (Courtesy of the Carolina Institute of Faith and Culture)*

CHAPTER TWO

Autumn 1964

NEARLY a year after the stern-faced woman took Lloyd away, someone else came into our lives and stayed but a short while. Call me paranoid, but it did seem that a lot of people came and went in Noble before I finally left in the summer of 1970 to attend college in a small city near Sanders, Indiana, where Michael's grandfather kept horses.

In truth, what with all the accidents, murders—small town America has its share of violence—and such, I've lost count of how many people have died or just disappeared during my youth. Some like Lloyd were taken away, but some just...vanished. They'd just up and poof, be gone. Now and then, you might mention someone's name to your friends, and they'd look at you with quizzical looks of confusion and say, "Who? Never heard of 'em."

There was this one kid who fell off a tractor while cultivating cornfields one day and ended up getting sliced and diced by the discs. While not a common occurrence, the incident didn't cause any eyebrows to be raised; after all, in farm country accidents happen all the time. The year we all entered Junior High I met a girl who seemed to come from nowhere and vanish before the end of Christmas break.

Of course, no eyebrows were ever raised in that situation either because Michael, Jase, and I were the only ones who could remember anything about her. And I mean, no one! Not our teachers, the principal, the jerk-in-the-pants cowboys at the Noble Horse Barns, not even Bud, one of the owners of Esposito's Pizza, remembered her. Poof. Gone. Truly forgotten.

My friends and I were anxiously waiting for school to start. As usual, Mom took my brother, sister, and me to Sears & Roebuck for our annual back to school shopping. I hated that trip. Every year she'd force us to try on stiff clothes that had a distinctive 'new clothes' odor to them, and make a big deal out of ensuring we had every conceivable school supply advertised on huge Back-to-School savings signs that seemed to spring up like corn stalks round about July. I never could rationalize in my mind how Mom ever saved any money what with how much she spent every year on our trip.

"Mom, can't I have something I like for a change?"

I asked some version of this question every year. Each time my inquiries were acknowledged with another adaptation of the same response. "You'll wear what I tell you to wear until you're old enough to buy your own clothes."

As I stood like a newly sunken post in the ground, looking at myself in the full-length mirror, unable to move in those dang Levi jeans she always made me wear, all I wanted to do was run away. I just knew everyone at school would be wearing those soft denim bell-bottoms all the cools wore down at the Blake Hotel, and they'd be laughing their butts off watching me do my Frankenstein walk down the halls.

"Aw heck, Mom," I remonstrated with a revitalized push. "Just one pair at least. It's *Junior High* for crying out loud."

"No," Mom pushed back with renewed decisiveness. "*I will not* have you running around town looking like a hippy. And don't cuss."

No, just look like a fool. I thought. *Damn it.*

Then my thoughts turned to Lloyd, and I stopped making a fuss. I wondered how he was doing and if he was somewhere trying on new clothes and getting ready for school. In the mirror, I imagined him standing in a store wearing stiff Levi's with a huge grin on his face, saying to a shadowed person nearby, "I like them. Thanks."

Dang it. Then I thought about Jase. He'd probably be starting school with the hand-me-downs from his older brother that had a distinctive overused smell to them. *Double dang it.*

"All right, Mom," I said as one vanquished not from without but within. "I guess they'll be okay."

I swore right there that by High School I'd be earning enough money to buy the clothes I wanted and hoped Jase would be able to do the same.

On the ride home from the mall, I wondered how Michael was fairing on his shopping trip to Indianapolis where his mother took him to a tailor for handstitched clothing.

"Man, I wish she'd just take me to Sears like your mom. I hate standing around having my clothes pinned; and that smelly old guy running that dang tape-measure all over my body a hundred times to get the measurements correct: it gives me the willies."

I guess when you're a kid, nothing satisfies you.

"Mom?"

"Yes, dear?" She sounded somewhat wary.

"What you going to do with my old clothes? They still fit."

Mom seemed to drop her guardedness and thought for a moment. "Probably give them to Goodwill. Why?"

"I just thought that since Jase and I are the same size, maybe he'd want them."

"Well, I don't see the harm in that." Then she smiled at me in a way she never had before. She repeated, to herself it seemed, "No harm at all."

Every year I'd have to clean out my closet and set aside some of my old clothes—usually the ones I didn't wear much—and take them down to the local Goodwill Store. All told, I ended up giving Jase two pairs of jeans—nicely broken in—five shirts, one suit, and my old dress shoes.

We were standing out back of the duplex where he lived over on Francis Street in the Noble Slums. I didn't want to embarrass his mother by giving the clothes to him inside, so we decided to make the transfer outside in private.

"Well, I don' know, just don' have no use for no suit. But thanks man."

"Aw heck, Jase, they're practically new and I never wear 'em anyway."

Jase was the only kid I knew who had never worn a suit; well, that is, aside from Lloyd. I imagined Jase in those dress slacks, white shirt and tie, dress jacket with his hair all slicked back, and I laughed. Jase looked at me with his redneck face (I could almost visualize a piece of hay sticking out of his mouth), and said, "What's so funny?" He was already trying on the dress jacket over his mangy muscle shirt for size. Seeing him like that—adding in his faded jeans and bare feet—

tightened my gut and I leaned against the wall of the utility shed for support to keep from falling. I was laughing so hard.

"Nothing man. It…" Now I was on my knees because he'd hunkered down and pulled a wild weed out of the ground and was chewing on it. "…looks fiiiiinnne."

He pulled the wetted weed out of his mouth, spat, and said, "You know, I worry 'bout you sometimes, bud."

The first day of school, only a few of the three hundred odd kids were wearing the soft-denim bell-bottoms. The rest of us spent the day stiff legging it up and down stairs from one class to another—except the rich kids like Michael who all looked rather out of place in their tailored or imported slacks. The kids like Jase didn't seem to notice anything concerning clothing because most of them were all worried about how hard the classes were going to be. (I should clarify that not all poor kids were in the basic classes: some were, but a few of them did achieve academically. One of the smartest kids in our class lived in the Noble Slums next door to Jase. At least then the public schools of Noble were a ladder for many.)

"Damn it, guys, we're going to get all split up now that yawl are going to be takin' them high level courses while I'm stuck in basic crap," Jase said scanning his course schedule.

Michael looked at his lunch, over-cooked peas, half-cooked potatoes, something on a half a burger bun the cooks called a pizza burger, and made a face.

"Here ya go, Michael." I tossed him one of the tuna sandwiches Mom still thought I liked. "Let me try that thing you have."

"No problem. Thanks."

Jase was sitting backwards, his elbows on the table chomping an apple and fretting about spending the day sitting in basic education classes with the other 'C' students.

"I'm gonna miss you guys."

"Aw heck, Jase, we still have shop class together." I was poking at the fake cheese and so-called Sloppy Joe meat on the half bun wondering if it was safe to eat.

Jase looked over at me and said, "I think I heard it moo, man."

"Gym class too, guys. Oh, and study hall. Counting lunch, we still get pretty much of the day together." Michael took his time eating the tuna sandwich, attempting to wash it down with chocolate milk.

"Yeah, Jase, and don't forget football practice." I thought the thing did moo, so I settled for the other tuna sandwich instead.

Come to find out we had a lot more classes together than Jase thought, which was fine by us; the only real differences being math and science. While Michael and I sat in some pre-Algebra seminar listening to the seven-fingered teacher droning on about stocks and bonds, Jase got to 'lazy it up' in reviews of multiplication and long division. He didn't know how good he had it.

I hated shop.

Jase and Michael were good with their hands. They could measure and cut and hammer spare pieces of wood for hours and end up with great looking birdhouses, furniture, or just about anything useful. My one project, a gun rack, looked like two slabs of wood nailed to two other slabs of wood. Sort of.

"What the heck is that thing?" Jase asked, putting the finishing touches on yet another intricately designed birdhouse.

"Gun rack." I said, admiring the finely carved lattice trimming he'd added to his new birdhouse.

Michael was over at a private bench working on some kind-of-box-thing with flashing lights and switches covering the front. There was some kind of 'feeder-tray,' he called it, attached to the bottom. Flipping a switch, a bunch of holed cards started moving forward and then sideways along an 'output' railing, he said it was, as the lights flashed madly.

"Oh. Yeah. I...a...yeah. Looks good, man," he said, watching the lights flash. The lights suddenly stopped, and I heard a 'bing' sound as a short piece of paper popped out of a slot. "Hmmm?"

"Say, what's it, Mikey?" Jase asked peeking over Michael's shoulder.

"Well, it's supposed to be the calculation of the amount of thrust and horizontal, tri-axle force needed to...."

"Oh...a, tri whatza?" Jase was scratching his head.

"...but the summation variance is..."

"Yeah. Okay then." Jase shrugged at me as he headed over to get a grade from the teacher for his birdhouse. Michael was a genius. He had an eidetic memory. Why his parents insisted he not be shoved ahead, say on to college, mystified not only me, but also every educator in the Noble public school system (or the entire Midwest, it seemed).

I couldn't even build a gun rack.

"Screw this crap," I said—a little louder than I'd meant—before tossing the *thing* I'd made into the garbage bin.

There was a back room connected to the shop area that no one used. The teacher called it dead storage. I figured it was just the place for me because I felt like deadwood. No matter how hard I tried, I just couldn't get the hang of building things. So, I grabbed my notebook and went into the storage room to write.

I'd been writing stories and poems since the fifth grade. I even won a prize once. Michael said that writing was my forte; Jase just said I was weird. Maybe I was. I did sometimes feel out of step with the rest of the students in our classes. While everyone sat around gossiping and carrying on, I'd sit with my notebook open watching them and making notes. The only people I could relate to were Jase and Michael, except when it came to shop class: then I really felt like an outsider. Even the girls in class were better at building than me.

"What the *heck* is this thing?"

Another kid yelled, "*Who* the heck built it?"

Dang it, I thought, *someone has found my gun rack.*

A girl's voice (I think it was Jenna, the girl from our sixth grade class, who the previous September had caught a case of lice) said, a bit too loudly I thought, "Three guesses, and the first two ain't Jason Quinn or Michael Bear."

I think even Michael and Jase were laughing.

God, I hated shop class.

Damn it. I kicked an old tarp and it fell to the floor in a heap of dust.

From a shadowy corner of the room, someone coughed.

"Did you have to stir up all that dust? Damn." She said, followed by a racking cough.

I flipped on the light and saw a girl I didn't know sitting in the corner coughing. I couldn't tell for sure, but I think she'd been crying.

"Turn off the light and get out," she sobbed through coughs.

"Sorry. I didn't know anyone was in here."

"Oh, poo, go away." She thrust her head onto her knees and started crying. "Leave me alone."

I knelt down and eyed her for a few minutes. She was short with long, bushy black hair. I reckoned she'd come from the other elementary school because I didn't recognize her. Not knowing what else to do, I said, "Hey. You okay?" *Duh, no.* I thought, mentally kicking myself. "What's wrong?"

She lifted her head and I finally got a better look. Almost as an involuntary impulse, I thought to myself, *Man, she is cute!* She seemed angelic to me with full lips and a round cherublike face. She also had green eyes that were immense and appeared to sparkle: perhaps it was the tears filling those orbs (as well as the substandard lighting), that made her eyes mysteriously aglint; anyway, at the time she was to me just *really cute.*

"I hate this stupid class," she half-quivered in a manner that gave her, in all her orbed and ocular beauty, a soft hint of tragedy. "Nothing I make is any good. Everybody laughs at me."

At the moment, they are laughing at me, I wanted to say, but didn't. I knew exactly how she felt.

"What's your name?" Duh again. Mentally, I think I felt my foot kicking me in the rear.

"Caitlyn." She said it softly, staring at me, her eyes watery but not blinking. I was taken with her, but before I could ask more stupid questions, she pointed behind me and asked, "What's *that?*"

Great, I thought, *someone's gone and brought in my gun rack.* I wasn't going to turn around so they could flaunt the thing in my face while laughing. Then Caitlyn stood up and walked across the room. My eyes followed her. She was standing in front of something big, her hands on her hips. I went over and stood beside her.

"What do you think it is?" She asked, to no one in particular.

I'd seen one before, in a book. Sitting on a table was a gray metal contraption with a big round disc on top, and a little box thing with rollers attached to a lever.

"Looks like an old manual printing press." I said, amazed.

"Think it works?" Caitlyn earlier had seemed so sorrowful and dreamy, ethereal and sad, as to appear languid. Now she looked more agile, fiddling with a box containing little pieces of metal.

"I don't know. It looks like it might work okay." I had moved a little closer to Caitlyn.

She smelled good, like honeysuckle. For the first time, I noticed a single blemish on her nose, which appeared to be spectacle marks left from eyeglasses. As she wiped away the tears, she must have put those inside her leather vest. I brushed my hand against hers, and it felt cool and smooth as I reached for the box she was holding.

"Of *course* it works. But you'll have to clean it up first."

Oh, crap.

The shop teacher, Mister Wood, was standing behind us. "You're welcome to use it if you want."

He came over, moved away the tarp, and rolled the table out of its hole. "Hasn't been used for five years." "Of course," he added casually, "no one's really been interested in printing since, oh, now what was her name? Hmm, doesn't matter."

He looked me directly in the eye and winked.

"I'm told you're a bit of a writer." I acknowledged the truth, and he continued: "You know, Benjamin Franklin was a printer. Started his own newspaper on a machine not dissimilar to this one."

Caitlyn started examining the machine getting her hands dirty, but not seeming to care. Despite not wearing her glasses, she seemed to see well enough. *She must be nearsighted*, I thought. For someone who hadn't known what the thing was, Caitlyn seemed pretty familiar with it already. I was becoming more impressed.

"You know," Mister Wood said, rubbing his chin, "we're getting ready to start the mock businesses soon. People are going to need advertisements, business cards, and such." He put his hands behind his back, eyes looking up at the ceiling, rocking up and down on his toes. "An enterprising person could take advantage of the situation, and," he cleared his throat, "quite possibly pull an 'A' out the hat so to speak."

"I'm game," I replied. I realized he'd probably seen the gun rack, and whatever Caitlyn had tried to build. I decided I should not pass up the opportunity.

I looked at Caitlyn who was smiling and nodding in the affirmative. *Praise God*, I must have thought, taking in her soft yet tumescent eyes, studying how her hair framed her face so perfectly. In retrospect, I'd never looked at a schoolgirl the way I did Caitlyn in that moment (and afterwards, I confess to stiff-legging it from shop class, but for different reasons other than new jeans). Hours after class, I dreamed of her orotund mouth, her wonderous lips, and wished Caitlyn had been around that summer for spin-the bottle over at Stacy's house.

"Fine, fine." Mister Wood said while I was preoccupied with nascent thoughts of lust and love. "Consider it your number one project. I'll requisition the ink and paper you'll need." Then he turned and wandered back towards the shop.

"All right, put that…whatever it is back in the trash, and both of you get back to work."

Caitlyn and I returned to class where the laughter had long ceased. I didn't see her again until shop period the next day. We spent the next two periods cleaning and adjusting the press getting it ready. While I did most of the wiping and oiling, Caitlyn got the die drawers cleaned out and organized; trust me, that in itself was a two-person job, but by the third day, everything was ready to start production. Besides the printing press and support equipment, there was also an electric paper cutting machine that Mister Wood showed me how to use. Caitlyn, oddly enough, picked up on the operational procedures simply by watching me.

Once word got around about the printing press, orders for stationary, business cards, and flyers started rolling in. I spent most of my lunch hour, and all of my study hall time, taking orders. One kid even wanted some of his poems printed up into a little booklet.

"Oh, sure," Caitlyn said, "that's easy."

She started rummaging around in the storage cabinets. "Where's that press and glue? Hmmm?"

She pulled out this 'thing' that was nothing more than a 9" square piece of steel that screwed down onto the base plate.

"First, we stack the printed pages in here, see?" Since we began working together, her movements and talk sometimes seemed more decisive, more confident. Once again, Caitlyn began to allure me, though she seemed innocent of any intent.

"Uh, okay," I said. Then it occurred to me, *she sure knows her way around this place.*

"Then," she continued. (I loved the way she drew out some vowels.) "You just turn this knob until everything is pressed together really tight. Brush on the glue and let it sit. Then we glue on the wrap-around cover and after everything's dry, we can go ahead and use the paper cutter to even it all out. Easy." As she spoke all this, Caitlyn's arms and hands were stained with inks and other solvents, but she seemed to beam out towards me. Probably, I stood before her like the pubescent idiot I undoubtedly was. I confess to thinking, *she really is cute when she is dirty.*

"Okay," she had on a black shop apron with a notepad stuck in the pocket, a pencil behind her ear, and half-moon wire rimmed glasses that sat on the end of her little nose, "I've set up three sets of business cards. *All,*" she drew out her consonants pretty well too, "you have to do is put in the paper and *pull* the lever. Then I'll cut them to size once you're done."

As I worked with her, I came to realize that Caitlyn was really something else. Smart, pretty, organized, okay, maybe a little *spooky* sometimes. Like the way she could have a tray of lettering setup in the time it took me to cut through a stack of papers.

"Look. It's easy. You just have to think backwards."

Algebra was easy. Thinking backwards wasn't. It took me an entire period to set up one block for a business card; took her the same amount of time to do six. So, we decided to let her do all the setting up and I'd do all the lever pulling. She also did all the cutting. She was fast on that thing. She could measure, adjust for size, press the two buttons and foot pedal to drop the blades, raise blades, readjust, and slice like a Master Butcher cutting beef.

Everything about the process was easy for Caitlyn, but I was not complaining. In fact, I liked printing. It was interesting, fun, got me away from the wood, and provided me a lot of up close and personal time with Caitlyn. It got me away from regular schoolwork, and I also made quite a bit of money charging for services.

"The Mediocre Express?" I proposed as the name for our mock corporation. "Mediocre Express?" She repeated it again. "Okay, deal."

She was the first, and probably the only, girl I ever knew who was easy to please. Indeed, she never debated the issue, or any issue. I'd make suggestions, and she'd say, "No problem. Easy."

One day I suggested we print up the Bible, just to see if she was really listening. Guess what she said. "Ummm, not so easy, but sure why not." Then she scrunched up her eyes and started going through the supplies, "I think we'll probably need about two gallons of ink...."

Yeah, you know I did, and this time I reared my foot back double far to make sure it hit my butt good and hard.

"I'm kidding Caitlyn."

"Oh." Nothing more, just a simple, Oh. I really did love the way her lush lips formed an 'O'.

One thing I could never figure out was why I could never find her anywhere else in the school.

"Aw heck, man, it's a big school. You probably just have conflicting schedules. Ever thought to just ask her to meet you someplace?" Jase said one day during lunch.

Duh.

"Dude's in love man," Michael said, poking at something that sort of resembled a chili dog, "you can't expect him to be able to think."

I tossed Michael a chicken salad sandwich.

One Friday, toward the end of the semester in shop class, I asked Caitlyn if she'd like to have pizza with Jase, Michael, and myself on Saturday night.

"Ummm, I don't know." She started tacking some materials we'd been printing up.

"Don't think of it as a *date*." I said trying to be cool. "Call it a *thank you* for helping me get through this class."

She looked at me, pushed her glasses up onto the bridge of her nose, and smiled. "*You* helped *me*." Pausing for a moment, chewing on her bottom lip, she added quickly before running off, "Sure, why not."

Okay, I thought, *now that was weird*. But I was happy.

"Is that a new shirt?" Michael asked me while we sat at a back table inside Esposito's.

"What's that smell?" Jase said, leaning across the table and sniffing at me like a dog checking out a 'bitch in heat.'

"Leave off, man." I pushed him away. My left leg was jingling up and down so fast that the table shook.

"Hey you." Caitlyn appeared and bounced into the booth next to me. I reached out for my glass of water and tipped it over.

"Whoa, there, steady dude!" Jase had jumped up onto the back of the seats just in time to miss being drenched. "Damn!"

Caitlyn sniffed, and raised an eyebrow. "What's that *smell?*"

Seeing my discomfort, Michael quickly said, "Oh, I let the guys try out my new aftershave."

My leg stopped shaking, but my palms were suddenly sweaty.

"Oh." There was that 'Oed' mouth again. My leg started jingling.

Caitlyn looked at me, smiled and asked, "You gotta go to the bathroom?"

Jase burst out laughing.

"Whaa...what?" I replied, grabbing my leg and trying to stop the movements.

"Your leg is wiggling like you have an urge."

Michael joined in with Jase.

"What'd I say?" Caitlyn had a look of utter innocence on her round, angelic face.

"No, I'm fine. Really."

"Oh."

"Pizza's ready and hot!" Bud, one of the owners of Esposito's Pizza Parlor, brought over a hot, freshly made pizza split into three parts. I remember how he used only the freshest ingredients—fresh mozzarella cheese he custom sliced for each pizza made, and a special sauce bought from a gourmet cook in Italy for five hundred dollars. I still contend that Bud's pizza is the best I've ever eaten: after all these years, nothing comes close. "Half pepperoni, and one-quarter sausage and onion for Jase, and one-quarter works for Michael. Your root beer will be right up."

Caitlyn was licking her lips in a way that suggested she hadn't eaten in days, or years.

"Mmmmm, that smells great," She said, looking at me with those big eyes as if saying, *cut me a slice please.*

I cut off a slice of pepperoni and transferred it to her plate. Naturally, the cheese, instead of cutting neatly stretched to the limit. She wrapped the cheese around a finger and broke it off before grabbing her slice.

"Thanks. I *love* pepperoni."

I never saw anyone devour a fresh-out-of-the-oven piece of pizza like she did. "Can I have more, please?"

"As much as you wish."

"Owwwieeee!" Jase had burned his mouth after taking too big a bite, and was downing his entire glass of root beer. "Damn, that's hot!"

Caitlyn was holding her plate out for slice number three.

Unlike Jase, Caitlyn seemed to inhale rather than chew the hot slices, which I thought of as a little odd.

After dinner we all walked Caitlyn home. I didn't mind Michael and Jase tagging along because I didn't relish the long walk back home after dropping Caitlyn off.

Caitlyn lived down by the Junior High, a half a mile east from the center of downtown. The three of us walked with her down the dark streets. Well, Jase and Michael followed us more like. Caitlyn and I were holding hands and chatting about our little enterprise. We turned down Moirai Street near the Junior High and Caitlyn stopped.

She turned, kissed me hard (and I mean, *hard*), and ran off without a word into the shadows. All I could do was stand there stiff-legged, looking on as she disappeared into the dark. Jase and Michael came up and bracketed me.

"She's one weird kid," Jase said.

"Odd," Michael added.

"Yeah."

We never saw her again.

All through the second semester, I roamed the halls and looked, but she was just gone. Without her, I lost interest in printing, although I did a few projects here and there, but somehow without Caitlyn at my side it just wasn't the same.

Lucky for me, I didn't have to take shop class, but was allowed—thanks in part to a note from Mister Wood to the art teacher—to enter art class, usually reserved for eighth graders, where I sat in the hall drawing perception pictures of lockers and doors, and people milling about. Jase loved shop and was busy learning how to use all the power tools. Michael finally got his *computer* to work properly and won the Science Fair.

"Probably moved away over Christmas," Michael said as we sat at our usual table poking at his lunch wondering how the other kids could eat that mystery meat and those half-cooked (or overcooked) vegetables.

"Yeah, I guess," I said over the roaring moos of something we came to call, *Cow-paddy on a slab*. "I just hoped she'd have sent a letter or something."

"Get it over it, bud," Jase advised around a mouthful of banana. "There are lots of girls out there."

Yeah, I thought, *but only one Caitlyn*.

CHAPTER THREE

DARK TRAILS

AS I WRITE this, with the wisdom of age and hindsight, all the events in my life seem finally to come together as the threads of a fine tapestry are carefully woven in order to create a landscape both alien and familiar to those who view it. Like most people, I have felt a bit lost in this mad confusion of life. I have always felt as if I belonged somewhere else. Now I am beginning to see more clearly how my anachronistic feelings have continued to steer me off course; keeping me from achieving my true goals in life. We never truly appreciate how much our close friendships keep us focused on living; helping us remain awake and not lost in the waking dream of what-ifs. Only near the end of life, when we have either drifted away from good friends, or they have continued to the new frontier ahead of us, do we really understand that which is most important for us all. The one true secret of all existence viewed only as short momentary glimpses that are ignored, or too soon forgotten.

Clotho, the spinner of fate's web, may seem cruel at times with the curves and misery we experience, but, if you believe in such things, she spends much of her time attempting to correct errors injected by the great adversary. Direct hands-on involvement is not usually needed, but at times she makes herself known—as do many of the other Angels of Light—for reasons that will never be known or understood by mortals. I never believed any of this until Michael brought me his journals and spent a week revealing things that until then I had viewed as myth, legend, or twisted lore. So, I now look into my past to see my present more clearly. As I review those events that helped to shape my friends and myself, the hidden images sharpen, and I am filled with clarity of thought.

The wolves howl across the lake. Another mist has formed on the still surface of the green water. Summer is ending.

By the time Michael, Jase and I were in Junior High, we'd made it a ritual always to go camping together down at Brown County State Park—a few miles east of our hometown of Noble, Indiana—during the major holidays from Memorial Day to Labor Day.

The horsemen's camp sits at the top of a mesa reached by a narrow two-mile-long two-lane road. The winding road continues for another two miles and splits twice: to the left leading down to Straw Valley and to the right leading to Lake Ogle. On the mesa are three large primitive and semi-primitive camps—two with indoor shower areas and flush toilets. The horsemen's camp was located in the center next to the General Store and the buffalo pens, near the Nature Center, before a new and larger camping area exclusively for the horsemen was built down in Straw Valley.

Every holiday weekend, either Michael's father or my father would take Jase, Michael and me along with our horses down on Friday after school. We usually arrived early enough to get a good spot down the slope from the general store close to the showers, which was good for me because I took so many. I really never understood how Michael and Jase got by with just one shower a day. Mom said I was obsessive, but the truth was I just didn't like being dirty. Michael's parents slept in the camper attached to their pickup, and my parents slept in one of those pull-along campers that folded out. Jase, Michael and me slept in an old US Army wall-tent that we called our Base Headquarters.

Sometimes, Michael's grandfather and great-grandmother Tava joined us at noon to take us down extra early to save spots for the horses and trailers.

By midnight, trucks pulling trailers would be arriving and unloading horses all over the area, squeezing in wherever they could get their trailers. Michael, Jase and I were usually too excited to sleep on Friday and would be up roaming around the camp until about four in the morning.

One of the things we enjoyed most about our camping trips was riding the trails. There are three main trails leading out of the horsemen's camp, and I don't know how many branches out in the woods. We'd head out on one of the trails then cut cross-country to see what we could find. My dad often got angry with us for trailblazing, but even when he was giving us a chewing out in front of Mom and everyone else—reminding us how dangerous it was to get off the trails—I could see a hint of a smile on his lips. Dad was a true woodsman and had grown up with Michael's father in Sanders. He and his friends, in their youth, knew just about every stick and tree in Brown and Monroe counties. Before his death, he took Michael, Jase and me aside and asked, "Did you ever see the rainbow at midnight?" Looking back all these years, I think I finally understand what he meant.

I figured he didn't really mind what we did, but in some ways worried about what we might run into out there on our own. Michael's dad just frowned and told us to listen to William, my father, because he knew these woods better than anyone and understood what he was talking about. We'd listen, say 'yes sir,' and do it again the first chance we got.

Maybe we should have listened to my dad a little better.

One of our favorite trails leading out of camp was the 'A' trail that wound north to an open field near the fire tower. At several points along the trail lay fallen trees that no one seemed to care about moving out of the way. Generally, people would just ride around them, but not us. We'd get our horses into a slow canter, side by side, and jump the trees while yelling, "Whaaaaaahoooo!"

People would hear us coming down that mile-long trail, and move aside letting us pass. There must have been about 15 of those trees to jump and by the time we'd reached the open field our horses were pretty tired, so we'd rest them a few minutes before continuing.

Michael's horse was a stallion with long mane and tail that he called Darkle because he was blacker than night. I said he looked like the horse Zorro rode. Jase rode a medium-sized pinto named Tonto that was so hyped up from show racing he often spun in circles when not walking or galloping along a trail. My horse was a half-quarter, half-appaloosa with a strawberry mane everyone at the barns said was crazy because he had pig-eyes (eyes with more of the white showing than was usual). I named him Lucky—my reasoning was that if everyone else thought the horse was crazy then he'd have to be lucky for me. In fact, I was the only person, besides girls I personally introduced him to, that could even get on the horse.

"Dang it, Jase," I said as we rested the horses in the field, "settle Tonto down will ya."

"Trying to, bud," Jase said, bailing to the ground, "but you know how he gets once I let him run."

Michael had turned his horse loose and it was placidly chomping grass a few feet away.

"Maybe if you'd stop running him in those stupid shows he wouldn't get wound up." Michael didn't approve of horse shows; he said they were a waste of time. But Jase was good and made a lot of money on weekends running the barrels, poles and rescue races, most of which his dad took to support his drinking habit.

"Where are we going this time?" I asked, scanning the trees a quarter mile across the field.

"Your lead, man," Michael and Jase said together.

I hated that. At home, Michael was more or less our leader; but in the woods, I was. I liked being the one to make decisions, but sometimes it got on my nerves. There would be times when we went camping that I'd be the one to disappear, often for hours. I loved riding alone in the woods. It was peaceful and I could think clearly. Most of my best stories were thought up while riding alone.

I stuck my foot in the stirrup and said, "Race." Lucky sprang into action just about the time I was swinging up into the saddle.

"Dang it!" Jase spat, grabbing his saddle horn and swinging from the ground into his saddle, as Tonto spun in a circle, before pursuing.

Michael just whistled to Darkle who turned so Michael could spring up on him from the rear, just like cowboys do in the movies, and dug in his heels.

Clouds of smoke sprang up behind us as we raced neck and neck across the short trail from tree line to tree line. Entering the trail, we took a hard turn and jumped a downed tree single file. "Whaaaaaahooooooo!"

The trail made a descent, and I slowed the pace to a canter. At the bottom, I saw a deer trail and headed into the forest. I'd never noticed this particular deer path before, even though we'd been riding trails for years. But I had an idea where it might lead.

A couple of miles or so in the direction we were going was Ogle Lake where most of the city folk came to fish and picnic. But in the woods, you can get off track and turned around pretty easily and fairly quickly.

The deer path got lost in the foliage, and I decided to let Lucky have his head. We wound our way through the woods, dodging tree limbs, up and down hills, for a long time. I figured we'd gone off our intended course because we should have been near the lake by then. Michael and Jase never said a word about our heading; they trusted me and my woods-sense enough to know that we'd eventually reach a familiar spot.

But as we wound deeper into the woods, I began to worry. Partly because I had no idea which way to go, but mostly because I could tell by the light coming through the trees that the sun was getting ready to go down. Just about the time I was ready to admit that we were lost, Lucky burst out of the woods onto a trail.

I let out my breath.

"Dang man," said Jase. "I was worried there for a minute." He hopped off his horse and loosened up the girth. "Shoulda known you never get lost."

"Yeah," I said looking to Michael who merely stared back with a dark look that told me he knew we were lost, but debating the issue would get us nowhere.

"Getting dark guys. Anyone have any cigars?" Michael said, breaking the awkward silence, looking around as if expecting to see something out of the ordinary. That was one of the few times in our travels I actually saw fear on his face.

We didn't smoke, but often used cigars on night rides to keep track of where people were. You could always tell, if you couldn't hear someone speaking or the creaking of the leather on their saddles, where they were by looking for the burning cherry of their cigar. Well, that and the smell. On moonlit nights, it's not too bad, but this was the dark of the moon and the night would be pitch black.

"No," I said, "I'm all out. Jase?"

"Tapped," he said, hunkering down to chew on a weed. Michael scanned the trail and looked through the trees. "This trail seems to run north and south. I say we go south."

Besides being a genius, Michael had this uncanny way of knowing direction that was a little unnatural. We could blindfold him, spin him in circles, and he could still get his bearings almost immediately. He also suffered from a rare eye disease that made it possible for him to see clearly in total darkness, but required him to wear glasses with dark lenses in the daytime to keep from being blinded.

He kicked Darkle and started down the trail at a walk, Jase and I following behind. As we rode, a fog began to form. It seemed to fall slowly from the trees and onto us. Soon, we were riding single file,

Michael in front, Jase in the middle, and me in the rear. The night, combined with the fog, brought my visibility to zero. After some time—I don't know how long because I didn't then, nor do I now, wear a watch—I called out to Michael to hold up. My rear was getting tired and I wanted to stop to stretch my legs. Michael didn't respond, so I called out again, louder, "Michael!"

The night was quiet. I couldn't hear the squeak of leather from their saddles, talking, or any animal noises. Even Lucky was quiet, which was very strange. When you're out in the woods at night, you can hear for quite a distance, and the night creatures seemed to fill the trees with their racket. However, on this night, I heard nothing. I felt as if a veil to another world had swallowed me, stranding me in a nowhere land someplace between shadows of reality and fantasy. I chided myself for thinking that the books I had read by Burroughs and Lovecraft somehow had too much truth in them. I've never been completely comfortable alone in the darkness, but when I was with my friends, I was usually the brave one. On this night, however, fear took hold of my mind. Suddenly, I felt a cold touch on my bare neck like icy fingers stroking my flesh. "Shades of the mind," I said under my breath. "I gotta stop reading those horror stories."

Like I said, I didn't normally dislike riding alone, but it was a different case when you're alone in the dark, lost and the usual noises you're used to hearing aren't there. The farthest I could see was Lucky's head, and I noticed that his ears were perked up like he was on edge. When horses get angry their ears lay back, almost flat, but when they sense something curious, their ears point forward and twitch back and forth. He jumped suddenly to the side, almost dislodging me from the saddle.

"Easy, Lucky," I said, glancing about nervously. "What is it?"

Brown County is known to have packs of wild dogs that roam the woods, and I feared that some might be near, the way Lucky was moving his head about. Wild dogs are like wolves: they'll track their prey in silence, giving warning they're near only when they attack. I took my Buck hunting knife out of its sheath and nudged Lucky on, keeping my ears open for the slightest hint of anything moving in through the forest. Then I heard (or thought I heard) soft singing like that of a heavenly choir floating on the fog.

"Michael! Jase!" I yelled, starting to shiver with nervousness. "Hey! Where are you?"

Still, I heard no response, just that eerie singing calling out to me.

It wasn't like them to just up and leave me, for any reason, especially in the middle of the woods at night. I began to wonder if they'd gone off the trail in the dark and fog, and we'd gone and got ourselves into a real mess, when I saw a light up ahead. Dad often told us stories about Witch Light or Fairy Fire that would appear from nowhere and lead astray lone woodsmen. "You have to be careful out in the woods, boys." He would say as the campfire crackled, "These woods have long memories and harbor things known only in folktales." We really should have taken his advice more seriously. I shrugged off the eerie feelings and forced myself to think more realistically.

I reasoned that I might be coming out into one of the primitive campsites. I'd certainly been riding long enough to have gone that far, so I dug my heels into Lucky's side urging him to go faster. The sooner I was back in camp the better. However, as I got closer to the light, I saw that it wasn't the camps, but a small log cabin sitting on the side of the trail.

I'd been all through those woods and never seen any cabins before. Oh, we'd find old foundations, and forgotten family graveyards, or the remnants of barns—but never a fully functional cabin.

I began thinking about how long I'd been riding and calculated how far I might have gone. *Could be*, I thought, *I got off on some fire trail and was near the outskirts of Nashville*. Nashville, Indiana, is a small town about two miles west of the main entrance to the park on Highway 46. Roughly six miles from our starting point. It was possible that I'd ridden that far. Well, I figured, might as well ask whoever lived in the cabin.

Right about the time I reined Lucky to a stop, the door of the cabin creaked open and this girl came out. She was beautiful, at least from what I could see of her in the shadowed doorway backlit by candlelight. She seemed about my height and age, with long flowing black hair with thin strands of silver in it, wearing a mid-length black and silver dress and soft black leather ankle boots that were covered in a lattice work of silver webs. Suddenly, some sort of porchlight must have struck on because I could see that her face was round; she smiled brightly, easing the tension.

"I bet you're lost, aren't you?" Her voice was like wind chimes tinkling in a light spring breeze.

"Yeah, I guess. My friends and I got turned around in the fog."

45

Then I asked, hopefully, "Have they come by here?"

"Nobody has been here for, oh," she stopped and seemed to consider this for a moment, but soon brushed it off with, "it doesn't matter." She stepped aside in the doorway. "My name's Cloe, come in and be at peace."

I felt that icy feeling racing through my veins again. Twice before I had felt such a sensation—in the principal's office when I was five and a couple of years before this strange night when that nice woman from social services took away Lloyd. Both of those women were named Cloe, too. I figured it must be some common name in southern Indiana, but somehow, as I recall, they had similar features and smiles that made the heart melt with a quiet calmness. I shrugged the idea off and dismounted. After tying Lucky's reins to a tree branch and loosening the saddle, I entered the cabin followed by the girl.

It was a cozy, if not mysterious, one-room cabin. The drapes and curtains covering the single window were black lace with silver strands that made a pattern that kind of reminded me of a spider's web. There was a small wooden table with two wooden chairs in the center of the room. A big black kettle, hanging from a rail above the fire in the fireplace, was bubbling with what I took to be a stew of some kind. The aroma of vegetables and spices cooking made my mouth water. The only other furniture in the place were an antique wardrobe and china cabinet that contained several pieces of regular looking dinnerware—plates, cups, saucers and bowls—and a single twin bed with a black quilt, black sheets and a fluffy pillow in a black case—all with the same silvery web-like pattern.

The girl, walking to the kettle and stirring the stew, said pleasantly: "Please have a seat. There's milk in the pitcher on the table."

"Thanks," I said, as I sat down and poured myself a glass.

As there wasn't much else to do, I made small talk, hoping I wouldn't say anything stupid and end up kicking myself in the butt like I had with Caitlyn almost a year previously. I had met her in wood shop in 7th grade and immediately fell in love. She possessed a strange aura around her that drew me in and made me feel at ease. When she vanished after the fall semester, I felt as if the best part of myself had been lost. In many ways, Cloe reminded me a great deal of Caitlyn. But at 14 a lot of girls seemed to be similar in appearance. Still, I couldn't stop staring at her, wondering…

"You live here alone?" I said, feeling my foot making contact with my tail.

"Sometimes," she replied. "Not often. I travel a lot."

I figured she was definitely not my age. But she looks so young, I thought.

Right about then she turned, smiled, and said: "Thank you."

I blinked.

No way could she have heard my thoughts. I took a long drink from my glass and shook my head. Dang it, I thought, I must be really tired. I probably only imagined she'd said anything in response to my thoughts.

"I hope you like vegetable pottage," she said as she laid out two bowls and filled them with stew. "Seems to be all I have at the moment. I never eat meat."

When I smelled her enticing stew, I couldn't have cared less. Besides, I was so hungry that I couldn't help diving in. It tasted similar to curried sauce, but had something that seemed more akin to the medieval aftertaste of a perpetual broth. Whatever it was, it was delicious.

"Takes the chill off?" She asked quietly, her brown eyes sparkling with a silvery light.

"Yeah. Thanks." I had been a little chilly come to think of it. The warmth of the room, combined with the stew, started making me feel warmer, relaxed.

She was looking at me as we ate. I swear her eyes, big round and brown, could see right into my soul. She was giving me one of those odd feelings I often got around Caitlyn—a kind of excited tingling sensation on the back of the neck. Moments later, I felt my eyelids droop.

"Perhaps you should lie down and get some rest."

"Ummm, yeah, maybe…" It was a good suggestion. I was out before finishing the words.

I dreamed of an endless field of honeysuckle. The air was warm, although I could see no sun. Before me was a large waterfall that seemed to reach to heaven. As I stood marveling at the wonder of the sparkling water as it fell into the lagoon beneath it, someone said my name. The words hung on the air like soft chimes. I turned and saw Caitlyn standing behind me, her long brown hair being tossed gently by a soft breeze, and her bright eyes drawing me towards her…but before I could respond, I awoke.

The sunlight was rushing in through the open window and I heard the roaring sounds of birdsong coming from the forest. My host was sitting at the table, her legs crossed casually at the knee, and knitting something with what looked like silver thread.

"Good morning. I trust your dreams were pleasant." Sensing my disorientation she added, "Nothing is ever lost, completely." Then she winked at me, and I felt myself smiling like Mona Lisa.

"Wha…what?" I felt woozy as if I'd been teleported from one location to another. I blinked as the room came into full focus.

"Your fate has yet to be measured fully." She said, handing me a glass of milk. "This will make you feel better."

"Thanks," I said, sipping the milk, as I stumbled to the chair by the table. I struggled to connect her words with my dream, but was unable to make the connection. Coming more fully awake, I asked, "What time is it?"

"Just a few minutes past dawn, you should have no trouble finding your way back now."

I thanked her for her kindness and she followed me outside. Climbing into my saddle I said, "Maybe I'll come back and visit sometime."

She just smiled and winked at me, saying in her musical voice, "Oh, we'll meet again, I'm sure."

I headed south on the trail at a gallop hoping to find some familiar signs that would lead me back to camp. About 15 minutes down the trail, I came to a crossroads with a sign in the middle. Two wooden placards were nailed on it. One pointed right, and read 'Lake Ogle'; the other pointed left and read 'Campgrounds'.

I headed up the left side. After about another 20 minutes or so, I came out on the eastern side of the first primitive camping area and breathed a sigh of relief. As I slowed Lucky to a walk, I hoped that Michael and Jase had made it back all right. As I turned towards the general store, I heard Jase call out, "Yo, man, where ya bin?"

You never heard anyone breathe a louder sigh of relief than I did at that moment. Michael and Jase were sitting on the limestone wall outside the store drinking chocolate milk and eating Twinkies.

"I'm glad to see you guys. What happened? Is my dad mad?" Of course he was, I thought.

"Don't know man," Michael said. "We were riding along, came to a sign that pointed the way here, and hit camp around midnight."

"What about my dad?" I was envisioning not only a chewing out, but possibly a demoralizing belt lashing.

"No problem, bud," Jase said. "Everybody was in bed when we got in, and we told your dad that you'd gone off on one of your early morning rides."

I sighed loud enough to make the dead bang on the walls for quiet. Michael was laughing his rear end off.

"Thanks guys."

I thought about telling them about the girl in the cabin, but decided to keep that experience to myself. Sometimes, you have to keep secrets from people, even your best friends.

"Where'd you get off to anyways?" asked Jase around a mouthful of squishy brown Twinkie.

"I must have gone off the trail and wandered around in circles or something."

Michael stopped laughing and gave me a look that said he knew I was lying. Then he smiled and said, "Whatever, man. You're here now."

As hard as I tried, I never was able to retrace my tracks and find that cabin with the strange girl again.

NOTE

First published in Mallorn *53 in the Spring 2012 volume. (Courtesy of the Tolkien Society, UK)*

CHAPTER FOUR

GHOST OF THE STORY

May 1966

MEMORIAL DAY weekend, 1966, was one vacation that got permanently burned into the minds of Jase, Michael, and me. Partly because of three girls we met while camping down at Brown County State Park, but mostly because of what happened to us on a long night trail through Hidden Valley and into the small hamlet of Story, Indiana.

Several times a year, usually during the major holidays beginning with Memorial Day, our fathers took us down to the state park in Brown County to go camping and horseback riding. Sometimes my brother and sister would come with us, but by 1966 my sister had graduated and was off at college in San Diego, and my brother was away on some backpacking excursion by himself. I think 1966 was the year he hiked through part of the Olympic National Forest in Washington state.

Michael's grandfather and grandmother picked the three of us up at the Noble Junior High School at lunchtime on Friday of the big weekend. Michael's father said he'd bring four of the horses down that evening after he finished at work, and Dad would bring the rest around midnight after he got in from a long haul of block to Illinois. Since it was one of the big holiday weekends, Michael's grandfather said he'd run us up to the park so we could grab some good sites near the showers, *thank God*, which would also give us time to get the camp set up properly and have a big pot of chili cooking and ready for everybody when they arrived.

It had been a pretty tough school year, and my friends and I were excited, and ready to get the heck out of Noble for a while and run wild, which was just what we did as soon as our tent was erected and our cots and bedrolls laid out.

We had an old Army wall-tent that easily housed six people. We used it to store a giant cooler that we kept filled with sodas, cold cuts, and cheese for snacking. We kept our clothes, adventuring gear, and daypacks with flashlights and first-aid kits in three official Army footlockers that had belonged to Dad when he served either in the Second Great War or the National Guard afterwards. Our saddles and tack were all laid out in another corner of the tent on a piece of plywood to keep it all dry in case of rain, which happened a lot on our campouts.

Tava busied herself getting the campfire set and the fixings for the chili prepared, while Michael's grandfather set up the little pull-behind camper and put a couple of cases of beer on ice.

"You boys don't get into trouble this time," he said while blending the watery ice and warm beers. His arm he used like a spoon, moving bottles and ice flakes like he was cooking soup. Michael's grandfather always said it made the beer colder. His fingers were evidently immune from frostbite. Keeping his eyes on his stirring, he added, "That stunt at the fire tower on Labor Day about got us all kicked out."

"Yes, grandpa," Michael said.

Jase and I smirked remembering the incident. We'd gone out around three in the morning on Friday night, climbed over the fence and scaled the rickety stairs to the ranger's lookout station at the top. While we were up there having a look-see, old Rex, the local head game warden, caught us and hauled our young butts to the jail in Nashville. Michael's dad was furious, but mine just sat in the outer office drinking coffee and chatting with old Rex, who'd tried for years to catch him poaching deer out of the park back when he was younger. We were sitting dejectedly in the cell waiting to be released when, after a while, Dad stood and said, "We'll see you boys in court in a few weeks," and left with Michael's dad and Rex. They kept us in that jail until Monday morning when they collected us on the way back to Noble with the horses.

"I mean it, boys," repeated Michael's grandpa. "No trouble this time."

"Yes, sir," we assured in unison.

Once the camp was ready, we set out on our Schwinn Stingray bikes to see if we could find any of our holiday friends in the campgrounds. We met a lot of girls over the years in Brown County, and always looked for them as soon as we could upon arrival. Most of the time, however, we met new girls which was fine by us.

Heading out of camp, we took the first fork to the left and headed down the main road two miles then down a long winding hill about two more miles down to the main entrance where the swimming pool was located. The ride down was always fun and exhilarating. We'd get going really fast and coast, flying down the hills at breakneck speed. I'm sure you can already guess what the ride up must have been like.

When we got to the pool the place was deserted, so we hung out by the ranger shack watching the arrival of horsemen and regular campers. After an hour of seeing various types of trucks—some with campers and others stuffed with kids and equipment—we decided to return to the campgrounds. Riding bikes up a two-mile hill is no easy chore. There are a few dips that allowed us to coast, but for the most part it was slow, tedious pedaling, most of which was accomplished standing up. The only thing keeping our minds from such hard-going tedium was the blaring of music from my transistor radio. The terrain of southern Indiana played havoc with reception, so we could only get two or three AM stations tuned in clear enough to at least enjoy the crackling sounds of the Beatles, Rolling Stones, and other bands making their mark on the rock and roll scene. We were all in pretty good shape, so the ordeal wasn't too bad. By the time we got back to the top and flat riding, we were drenched with sweat.

"Okay, guys," I said as Mick Jagger's voice, which moments before had been distorted and seemed to hiss, now clearly sang "Not Fade Away." "Let's shower and go back out."

"Why?" Jase and Michael said together. "By the time we get back to the camps, we'll be all cooled off."

Yeah, I thought as Mick sang on about how 'love is love...more than one day,' *but I still want to take a shower and change clothes.*

I brought enough clothes to change three times a day. In contrast, Michael and Jase brought two pairs of pants and two shirts apiece. Honestly, I didn't know how they could stand it.

By the time we got back to camp, Michael's dad was there and had our horses unloaded. He'd come up from Noble by way of Highway 37 and entered the park from the side entrance, which was how he had been able to arrive without us passing him.

After we parked our bikes, I showered and freshened up, while Michael and Jase watered the horses, then we took off again, this time on foot to hang out at the nature center. The nature center is about a quarter mile walk past the buffalo pens down a little dirt trail. Jase kicked up quite a dust storm on the way. I think he did it on purpose just to get me dirty again.

"Damn it, Jase," I said, "I'm going to start calling you Pigpen."

"Deal with it, bud. Time you stopped being so damn prissy."

I wasn't prissy. I just wanted to look presentable in case we came across any interesting girls.

At home Michael usually wore suits to school, but had recently taken to wearing black t-shirts, jeans, and sneakers as casual wear. He said he got the idea from Einstein, but Jase and I believed he was copying the college beatniks who sipped espresso in our local coffee shop and read poetry by Allen Ginsberg or Frank O'Hara. (Michael could have also gotten the fashion idea from watching Zorro movies on Saturday mornings.)

Jase just wore any old bellbottoms that still fit, muscle shirts, and ragged sneakers. Unlike Michael, he had grown his hair long like a California hippie. He looked like a cross between Geronimo and some reject from "Leave to Beaver." My hair was long, though it only hung past my ears, and was covered by my black felt wide-brimmed hat. My shirts were neatly pressed snap-button western style tucked neatly into boot-cut jeans that covered the tops of my brown swede Dingo boots.

I was just neat, not prissy.

As we approached the nature center, we saw three girls of about our age. Near the parking lot, they sat together at a picnic table in the small field under some trees. Even from fifty yards, we could see them clearly. One was a blonde, one a brunette, and a third had reddish-brown hair that was bushy and a little curly that hung almost to her waist. As we walked, side-by-side towards them, I felt the familiar pounding of my heart in anticipation of meeting new girls.

I was usually shy at school. Many of the girls in our classes took my shyness to mean that I was a snob, standoffish, or arrogant. Truth was, girls made me nervous—except for Caitlyn, which was probably why we got along so well. For some reason, when I was with Caitlyn, I felt comfortable and accepted. Michael said that she and I were twin souls; Jase said we were both weird, so we fit together. However, when it came to other girls, I turned to water: but not down at the park. In Brown County, I felt confident, in control, and cared nothing what people thought about me because I could always disappear into the woods on my horse if I got too uncomfortable. Even so, whenever I was about to meet new girls, my heart palpitated, and I'd feel a deep tintinnabulation within me.

Jase and Michael, probably echoing their parents, both said it was my hormones getting excited. There was truth in this since I did end up getting stiff in the leg quite a bit camping. However, I still think there was something more to it.

"I want the blonde," Jase said.

"Long haired with curls for me," Michael added.

Damn it. I thought. *Are we going to end up fighting over some girl?*

This was the first time that any of us had fixated on the same girl. Usually when we met girls, we'd talk them up and let pairings happen in a natural manner.

Jase preferred a rough, get-your-hands-dirty type; Michael liked girls with light hair and big eyes; and I went for the brainy type. That said, a piquant pair of feminine eyes allured me quite easily, and the bushy-headed girl had the biggest eyes: she reminded me a lot of Caitlyn—*my* Caitlyn, not Michael's.

The hell with it, I thought, *I'm an idiot.* I decided if Michael wanted her, I would not fight with him. I'd flirt with the dark-haired girl for a day or so.

Still, I considered if this were the same girl. The chances of that girl actually being Caitlyn were remote, very remote. *Still*, I thought, *what if.* Of course, at that moment my hormones didn't know up from down, but my heart was unsure.

Michael is compellingly smart, and he could take a face he saw and age or de-age it in his head. I'm sure he'd done that to the bushy-headed girl and determined that she wasn't Caitlyn.

If she had been, he wouldn't have hesitated to tell me.

As things turned out, we didn't have to do any fighting for her attention. As the three of us approached their table the bushy-head girl stepped off, walked up to me, and said, "Hey you."

I blinked. Stunned into silence, I felt my right leg start to jingle. I took a better look at her round brown face framed by the long hair with bangs cut just above her eyebrows. The black tank-top showed a portion of her flexuous belly and her blue bellbottoms neatly covered her small bare feet. A rush of honeysuckle filed my nostrils and I blinked again. She stood straight, looking hard into my eyes. She raked short brown fingers through her hair, just like Caitlyn used to, and smiled, as she said, "What's wrong with your leg? You have an urge?"

Her voice was familiar, too familiar. I lost myself in her sparkling gaze. Her eyes were so blue I felt like I was floating in an ocean of sensual perfection.

"Sorry," I said, though with less embarrassment here than had we been at school or anywhere in Noble. "My leg does that sometimes."

"*Oh.*" She replied, making a really cute 'O' with her full lips.

I melted.

What else could I do? She reminded me so much of Caitlyn.

Then she stuck out her hand and said, "Hi. I'm Jaid."

When she said her name, I swallowed hard and kind of felt a quick rush of cool racing through my body. It wasn't a rush of excitement, but of disappointment. Yes, the chances had been astronomical. My leg, however, wouldn't stop jingling.

"If you need to pee," she laughed, "just pop off behind a tree. I promise not to peek…much."

I grabbed my leg and forced it to stop. When Caitlyn had noticed my leg jingling, she also thought it meant I needed to rush to the toilet. *Damn,* I thought, *girls really do think the same.*

"You want to go for a ride?" My words came out a little shaky, but her reply was quick and smooth.

"Yes," she said with without hesitation, and then added this rejoinder: "As long as it's on a horse and not some narrow banana seat on some rickety bicycle."

We left the others at the nature center and walked back to camp to get Lucky and take a ride together. Along the way, Jaid kicked up a small dust storm, but this time it didn't bother me. Her hand found mine and we laced our fingers. I felt a calm I had not known since Caitlyn wash over me. Jaid chatted on nonstop about something, but I wasn't paying attention. I just listened to the sound of her soft voice and relished the cool feeling of her skin against mine.

Once in camp, I prepped Lucky and swung into the saddle; Jaid was up behind me with her arms around my waist before I knew what was happening.

I always tied my denim jacket on the back of the saddle so it made a kind of second seat, allowing girls to sit right up on me, or if I was on the back, me on them. She squeezed up close and whispered in my ear, "Let's get lost together."

"Where the heck you been?" Michael asked as I walked slowly back into camp, leading Lucky.

"Yeah, man, chili's been ready for two hours," Jase added from a nearby log, spooning in a wad of chili and taking a bite off a piece of bread.

I wanted to say that I had taken Jaid down to Straw Lake, and made-out with her, going all the way to third base in fact. But I kept quiet. First of all, it was not any of their business, and secondly, it was not any of their business. Instead, I tied up Lucky, removed the bridle and saddle, watered him, and went to take a really cold shower, stiff legging it all the time of course.

"I need a shower," was all I said.

Jase and Michael laughed. Then Michael locked his gaze on me. I'm telling you, whenever he did that, I got unsettled. It seemed the older we got, the more mysterious he became.

After my shower I joined the others for a quick dinner, washing the chili down with cold root beer.

"We're meeting Nelda and her friend Vicki, that's the one with dark hair, at nine for a night ride." Michael said, looking at me curiously. "You coming?"

"Um, yeah, I guess," I said, thinking about Jaid.

Right about then, a sweet voice said from behind me, "Hey you."

I turned and saw Jaid smiling. She walked right on up to me, smiled and kissed me on the lips. Michael and Jase gaped. Grandma Tava came over with a bowl of chili and said to Jaid, "Would you like some chili, dear?"

"Ummm, thanks. I *love* chili." *Lord,* I thought, *I love the way she draws out her vowels.*

I couldn't take my eyes off of Jaid. She had on the same thin muscle shirt that provided a perfect view of her form and neck, all of which seemed embrowned of countless summers. I also noticed a hickey I'd given her by the lake. At that moment, I suddenly saw her as a concinnity of feminine perfection, and this made me contrite for causing a blemish; I wondered if she resented me (even if just a little) despite her outward friendliness. Once she hitched up her too-big-bellbottoms and sat next to me, my worries were allayed.

"Dear, dear, young lady," Tava said, not unkindly, "you really should wear shoes around here."

"Oh," Jaid said unfazed, "I never wear shoes except when I really have to."

Suddenly, I was ebulliently hot all over. Sometimes these reactions happened to me, and I knew from experience that my face was beet red, perhaps also rutilant from both color and sweat.

I considered how I might deflect attention from my florid complexion when Jase burst out with, "Holy cow! You get bitten by some giant mosquito or something?"

Oh damn.

Jaid just smiled, eating her chili, and winked at me. "Something like that."

She just automatically fit-in with us.

"Hi," Michael said casually. "I'm Michael, and the one with no manners is Jase, in case you forgot us since seventh grade."

"I's gots manners." Everyone, Tava, Michael's grandfather and Dad included, burst out laughing.

"Hi all," Jaid said smiling, "I'm Jaid."

Michael and Jase looked at me and raised their eyebrows.

Everyone has a double somewhere, although I doubt two unrelated people could be near perfect copies of each other. There was a moment down at the lake when Jaid was lying beneath me that I was sure Caitlyn's face was looking at me. At the time I thought it had to do with the way her hair was all splayed out and the early shadows partially covered her features that gave me such an impression. The ease with which Jaid opened up to me and acted so relaxed around my friends made me feel as if we'd known each other for years.

Michael said I had my first experience with love at first sight. That remark made me wonder if I was attracted to Jaid for the right reasons.

"You two look good together." Michael said casually trying to divert any prying eyes from me or Jaid's neck. "Must be love at first sight. True love. The kind shared by true soul mates."

Jaid put her arm around my shoulders and shot back with, "Just a couple of lost souls catching up with each other in a new life." Then she winked at Michael.

"I don't believe in reincarnation." Michael's voice had taken on its serious tone. "I was just making an observation."

"Maybe you should," she responded with summer confidence that seemed to provide her immunity from Michael's gazes or the susurrous suspicions of others in our camp.

"Who cares?" Jase interrupted. "What's important is we have to meet the girls in an hour. So, let's focus on that."

"Well then," Jaid said who persisted in her untoward (though not unwarm) manner, "I have time for more chili."

We saddled the horses, and I let Jaid get up front as I swung up behind her. "Let's go, guys."

Michael's Dad said, "You boys be careful."

"All right," Michael said, kicking Darkle and leading the way to the nature center. "Most likely we'll be back late since we're going to Story through Hidden Valley."

After picking up Nelda and Vicki at the nature center, we headed down the "C" trail towards Hidden Valley. "Should get there around midnight or so," Michael said. "We'll take a break in Hidden Valley and get some drinks."

The ride from the camps to Story was roughly a six-hour round trip. We'd taken the trail several times, usually with large groups of other riders, but this was our first solo excursion. As we rode, I wrapped my arms around Jaid, and she leaned back against me, allowing me to gently kiss her neck. We rode single file with Michael and Vicki in the lead. I could hear Michael and Jase talking to the girls as we wound deeper into the woods. Jaid put her hand on my thigh, rubbed it and said, "I love the way you kiss me like that."

I felt like we were alone in the universe.

We rode, mostly in silence, for the better part of two hours, then Michael yelled, "Hey, we're coming to Hidden Valley. Better zip up!"

Jaid laughed and yelled back, "Just go on ahead, we'll be there directly."

Hidden Valley is a little place down on the flats. There are a few farms in the area, and a refreshment stand owned by a retired couple named Betty and Ralph Smith. The trail we were on opened out into a wide field next to the old two-story farmhouse where the Smiths lived. They'd set up the refreshment stand as a courtesy to riders, and there were a lot of riders who passed through on holiday weekends. A two-lane dirt road led south out of the Smith's place and crossed the main road about three miles down, past a place called the Tobacco Barn.

As we came into the area of the refreshment stand, we saw the lights on and several other horses tied up to the hitching rails.

"Looks like there's a crowd here already," Jaid said as we dismounted and stretched our legs.

"Yeah," I said. "Most people like to take this trail the first night out."

We tied Lucky up and went to get a couple of sodas. Michael and Vicki were sitting together talking, while Jase and Nelda sat on one of the picnic tables kissing. It looked like Nelda had taken a mouthful of water and was dripping it out as they kissed. Jaid nudged me and said, "Now that's what I call a sloppy kiss."

The Smiths were sitting in their lawn chair recliners drinking beer as their oldest daughter served customers. Some riders we knew came and went, and we all exchanged greetings while chatting with Betty and Ralph. Mister Smith liked to tell stories, and the one he told us that night was a zinger.

"Oh yup, I remember when your Dad [indicating me] and I went hunting for that panther; oh, when was that?"

"Forty-three. Dear," Betty added.

"Oh yes, forty-three. Well, boys let me tell you, that was one night I won't ever forget." He leaned forward for emphasis, "We'd gotten separated, and I come out of the woods up round the 'bacco barn and heard the most hair-raising scream anyone's ever heard."

"A woman is said to be haunting the woods around here," Betty interjected.

"I was getting to that."

"Sorry, dear. Please go on."

"Well, I stopped dead in my tracks and cocked my head. Then I heard it again. Like a woman screaming in utter anguish. Well, it scared me, but then I thought that's how a wildcat sounds out here in the woods, and figured your pappy had done got the beast. But I hadn't heard a shot."

"That wasn't no wildcat they were after boys. It was a witch. She'd been known to change into a black panther and bother the livestock."

"Who's telling this story?"

"Sorry, dear."

"Anyway, I hear a gunshot and a few minutes later your pappy comes out of the woods saying he'd gotten the panther. I said, well you sure? And he shows me a paw, and says, 'Oh yeah.' Well, about that time we hears this wild scream, and we both turn white as sheets in the snow. Your pappy throws the paw into the woods and we beat it on out of thar."

"Next day, old Missus Warten, the woman everybody said was a witch, had her left arm all wrapped up in bandages and said she'd got her hand cut off trying to fix some machinery on her farm."

"Betty, you're getting ahead of me."

"Go on, dear."

"Well, anyway, a few days later Missus Warten disappeared and hasn't been seen since. But—"

"Sometimes on nights like this you can hear her screaming out in the woods."

"So they say."

Michael had his arms around Vicki, who was visibly tremulous, and Nelda nudged up closer, if it were possible, to Jase who merely laughed. I looked at Jaid, expecting to see her a little shaken, but she didn't seem unsettled at all.

"Oh poo," she said. "There's no such things as witches or spooks."

Ralph looked at Jaid, a bit oddly I thought, and said, "Well, young lady, that ole witch ain't the only thing spooking these hollers. Y'all know about the ghosts haunting Story?"

We shook our heads.

"Well, you just keep close together and keep your eyes open when you're riding down the road. You just might see something out of the ordinary."

Betty also looked at Jaid rather oddly, saying, "Supposed to be the ghost of a young girl haunting the park. Some folks say she's the daughter of the ghosts down at the Story General Store."

Jaid nudged closer to me and said in a whisper, "Okay, now I'm getting scared."

To be honest, I wasn't feeling so brave myself. Then Michael said, "Ghosts are nothing to worry about. They can't harm you. That's what grandfather and Tava say."

"True enough, Michael," Ralph said, still looking oddly at Jaid, "Most people harm themselves running away in fright."

Then we heard a sharp high-pitched scream and jerked around.

"Sorry folks," the Smith's daughter said from the concession stand. "I just burned myself."

"Best put some butter on it dear," Betty said, not taking her eyes off Jaid.

We thanked the Smiths and took our leave of them. We rode in silence down the dirt road past the tobacco barn. Somehow, the night seemed darker, the trees closer, the horses more jittery…especially, the closer we came to the barn.

The old tobacco barn sat on the east side of the trail, partially up a slight slope. The gray rotting boarding of the barn was overgrown with weeds, brambles and young trees that grew out of it thick as July corn. The old barn had been used at one time to store and dry the cut tobacco but now was dying the death of forgotten rural dwellings. On the west side of the trail was a wide field containing fifty acres of tobacco growing green and tall.

A million stars twinkled at us from the sky; the moon had yet to rise. Although our eyes had adjusted to the evening darkness, it was difficult to keep track of the horses in front of us. I could see Tonto's white spots as he pranced about looking as though he would burst into a run at any moment. Jase was on the front now, with Nelda snuggled up behind him holding on like a frightened cat clinging to a tree. Michael and Vicki's voices floated on the air in whispers. Jaid rode behind me, her fingers tangled tightly around my belt.

Although I'd ridden many trails at night, sometimes alone, for some reason I felt nervous. It was a feeling I could not put my finger on and hold down. Ralph's story was playing tricks on my mind, probably on all of our minds, and I twitched at nearly every little night crackle from the nearby woods.

As we rode past the dying barn, something jumped up out of the interior and screeched before darting off into the woods. Lucky jumped quickly to the right nearly dislodging us.

"What the heck was that?" Jaid said, pressing up closer to me.

"Just a racoon," I said, hoping I was right.

From ahead of us, we heard a scream and Jase yelling for Tonto to steady down. Then Michael yelled back at us, "Did you guys see that?"

"What?" I yelled, wondering what the heck he could be talking about.

"Something on two legs just ran out of the field and across the trail!"

"Yeah," Jase yelled, "we saw it, damn near ran us off the road."

I could feel Jaid trembling behind me. Heck, it felt like she was trying to crawl up inside my back pocket. Kicking Lucky, I urged him forward to catch up with the rest just about the time a piercing scream erupted out of the woods. I turned my head in the direction of the scream and, I *swear* I saw two red eyes looking at me from out of the darkness.

"Get on up there, Lucky!" I kicked him again, getting him into a fast canter. "Michael! Hold up!"

As we caught up to the others, they too started off to keep pace. We rode like that all the way to where the dirt road intersected the main road and stopped.

"Damn, guys, did you see that thing in the woods?" I said, just a tad out of breath.

"Nope," everyone said together. "Don't want to either."

We heard another scream and looked at each other.

"What you think that was Michael?" Jase said, standing on the road holding Tonto as still as he was able.

Michael frowned. "Wildcat. Just a wildcat."

The girls were getting scared, except for Jaid who was silent and started looking a little pale I thought.

"No wildcat I ever heard of walks on two legs!" Nelda said a tad too loudly.

"Come on guys, let's go! Let's go!" Vicki was saying from behind Michael.

I touched Jaid's hand; it was cold as ice. I whispered to her that we were okay now, that we'd reached the road, but she didn't answer. There really wasn't much to be scared of in those woods, day or night, except packs of wild dogs, and we'd never heard of anyone, especially in a group, being bothered by dogs for almost two years. What the others thought they saw back on the road had likely just been a deer. Running the way deer tend to run, and it being dark with our imaginations running wild, it was amazing they hadn't imagined seeing Bigfoot.

"Let's get on up to the store, guys." I said, turning Lucky down the blacktop towards Story.

The steel shoes on the horse's hooves made a loud clacking noise that I was sure would wake everybody in that little hamlet out of a sound sleep as we rode down the road. Even though it was near one in the morning, I saw a light on in the general store, and relaxed somewhat as we saw two streetlights come on out front.

"Looks like someone's still up in the store," Michael said, helping Vicki to the ground and tying Darkle up at the railing. "Anyone need to go before we head back?"

"I think I already did," Jase said, breaking the tension that for the better part of an hour had kept everyone silent.

The inside of the store smelled musty as we entered, the wooden flooring creaking a bit too loudly in the night. Near the counter was a nice-looking middle-aged couple. The man, tall and slightly balding, wore an old-style shopkeeper's apron and smiled at us as we filed inside. His wife had beautiful long red hair and wore an old-fashioned blue frock. She sat in a weathered rocking chair knitting. When she saw Jaid, she said, "Well, dear, finally decide to come on home. We've been waiting up. Who're your friends?"

We'd been past that old store a number of times before, but never when it was opened at night. The elderly couple standing before us this night we'd never seen on any of our previous trips during the daytime. I guessed the folks working the store during the day were either locals or the couple's older children.

"Sorry, Mother." Jaid walked over and gave the woman a kiss on the cheek. "I took a hike up to the main camps, and this nice boy brought me back on his horse."

"Well," the man said smiling, "just let us know next time sweetheart. You know how your mother worries."

"You is the one who worries," the woman said, winking at me.

Jaid gave me a kiss and said, "I better get on to bed. Maybe I'll see you tomorrow."

"Sure," I replied, confused.

The ride back to camp went by without us hearing anymore screaming or seeing strange creatures running amok through the trees. As we rode into camp, after dropping Vicki and Nelda off at their tent, we saw Dad sitting up with Tava; they were drinking beer and chatting.

"You boys have a good ride?"

"Yes, Dad," I said, settling Lucky in for the night. "We took a ride down to Story and had a nice chat with the couple who own the store."

Tava sat in her rocking chair and looked at me with a broad smile. Dad said, "Can't see how that could happen, seeing how's they just left here a few minutes ago. They've been here since about ten or so."

Michael looked at Jase who looked at me as Tava started laughing. We never saw Jaid again.

SECOND PHASE

AGLINT IN SUN

CHAPTER FIVE

Autumn 1968

IN the 1960s, there wasn't much for teenagers to do in Noble on Friday or Saturday nights aside from sitting in the parking lot of Esposito's Pizza and watching girls walk by while idly chatting with your friends about nothing of importance. For boys lucky enough to have a car and steady girlfriend, there were plenty of isolated areas on the backroads leading into the heavily forested lands of southern Indiana where, quite often, more than friendly necking and touching occurred.

But something downtown Noble had was the local theater—The Themis—where teenagers went for double features (tickets were less than a dollar) and make-out trysts in the balcony. My friends and I weren't always 'four-leaf clover lucky.' Well, except for Michael who was golden five-leaf clover lucky most of the time.

"What ya want to do tonight, Jase?" The question—more of an inceptive statement than an inquiry in earnest—was our signal. For us, these weekend musings became something of a liturgy.

Jase shrugged. "Reckon go on down to the Themis and see a movie. I hear there's a good horror flick on tonight." He turned to Michael, who was sitting on the hood of his new 1969 GTX. "Hey, ya coming or what?"

"I guess," he called back in an almost disinterested manner. With the passing of each day, Michael seemed to grow more mysterious. At times, he appeared to exist apart from the universe we shared.

After some ritualized back and forth, my two friends and I usually chose The Themis most Friday nights where we watched movies and tried to pick up girls. Besides Esposito's parking lot, the theater was the best place to meet unattached girls, especially during scary shows. Indeed, picking up girls at scary movies seemed easy. You went in early, got some popcorn, found a seat up in the back row, and waited for the theater to fill up.

Boys and girls with dates always went up to the balcony seats, and the single girls, usually in groups of two to four, sat in the middle and towards the front of the regular seating area. The easiest targets were the ones who sat directly in the row in front of you; I remember those nights where all I had to do was lean forward a little and chat them up.

As teenagers in a small town, most of us were at least acquainted with each other. However, the magic of a local cinema—with its big screens, deep sounds, buttery popcorn smells, and dark isles speckled with pinpricks of light—often infuses the familiar with mystery and creates anticipation. When Noble boys and girls entered The Themis, all that appeared familiar became, for us, wondrous and strange; it seemed magical, and this compounded the expectations we brought.

Once the movie started to get scary, you were pretty much assured of an invite to join them. However, two girls sitting alone in the middle or up closer were easy to hook-up with as well. All you did was let the movie start, feign going to the bathroom, come back and sit on either side of them. Most of the time, it worked for me. Girls just seemed to prefer hugging onto a guy during the scary parts rather than each other. Once you were sitting with them, it didn't take long before the kissing and touching began.

According to Michael, the girls planned it that way. "If they play hard to get, and the guy approaches them anyways, they figure he's worth their time." Of course, romantic movies were good for picking girls up as well. As Michael said, "All you have to do is sit near them and act sensitive or offer a shoulder for their tears and you were home free." True or not, I tended to believe Michael when he professed to know something about the opposite sex.

"Not much of a crowd tonight." Jase said, sitting with his sneakers up on the back of a chair in the row of seats in front of us, while crunching his popcorn.

"There's Jenna and Tippy," Michael laughed, indicating two girls just walking in and sitting up in the middle rows. "Go talk to them, Jase."

"Aw, heck man," Jase said punching Michael in the arm. "Don't you like cootie girl?"

"Stop it guys." Jenna had actually started to fill out rather nicely, and I hated how both of Jase and Michael still held that one lice incident against her. "Jenna's cool." Besides, I knew for a fact that Jase and Tippy had made out more than a few times, and not just at the movies. "That was years ago. Give it a rest."

At sixteen, Jenna was looking pretty good to me. She stood nearly five-eight in her socks and had a head of lush blonde hair that looked like newly-sprouted corn silk. It was long, straight, and bright yellow, the color making her blue eyes seem to shimmer like sapphires in the sunlight. I remember feeling puzzled about how a girl in grade school wouldn't get a second look, but in high school those Plain Janes burst from their shells looking not only pretty but damn near gorgeous. At the time, it was enigmatic.

After her family had all that trouble with their well water, Jenna's father sold the farm and moved them to a little cracker-box house on Parcae Avenue near the railroad tracks that ran through the town. As far as I knew, she never had lice after that.

"Come on, Jase," I said, ready for the show (and I wasn't thinking of the film) to commence. "Let's go talk to them. Later, Mikey."

Jase gave Michael another punch on the arm just for the hell of it.

"Later losers." Michael said, leaning back in his seat with a dark look on his face.

Sometimes I couldn't figure Michael out.

Jase and I ended up walking Jenna and Tippy home after the movies because Michael left early, and at the time, he was the only one in our group with a car. I didn't blame him for being angry at us. We'd been friends since kindergarten, and friends don't just up and desert each other like Jase and I had done to Michael.

"Aw hell man," said Jase casually, "stop fretting about Michael, he's okay. Probably just down at Esposito's looking at girls." He talked on as we walked down the dark streets behind Jenna and Tippy. "It's not like there were any other available girls around the theater tonight."

Jase was right. The crowd had been light for a Friday. I figured Michael decided to peruse the pizza lot to see what he could find. As we turned off Main Street onto a side road leading to Parcae Avenue, I heard the distinctive roar of dual exhaust as his GTX pulled up behind us.

"Hey guys, want a lift?"

Great, I thought, *now Jenna's gonna get all gushy over Michael because of his car.*

"No thanks." My heart leapt when Jenna brushed him off and kept walking, glancing at me with a look that seemed to say, *let's get out of here.*

"Thanks, Michael," Jase said, his arm around Tippy as they headed off into the shadows of the train depot. "I guess we'll see you tomorrow."

"Later guys." Michael smiled and winked at me as he gunned the engine and roared off.

***

"So, how'd you two do last night? Either of you get laid?"

We were out at the Noble Horse Barns cleaning stalls early Saturday morning when Michael strolled in to feed his horse. I sometimes hated his disenchanting manner of speech, especially about our teenaged romantic encounters.

"None of your business," said Jase whipping dirt and sweat out of his face as he bent to shovel out more manure.

"That necklace of yours says different." Michael smirked grabbing a five-gallon bucket and starting to fill it with water. I kept shoveling to ignore them.

Truth was Jenna and I had spent the entire night together. Once we arrived at her house, she invited me in. "My parents are gone for the weekend. I'm alone and that movie scared me." She batted her eyes and squeezed my hand in a manner that was alluring (if not entirely convincing). "You want to stay and make sure I'm okay?"

Of course, my heart raced like a lightning bolt. I imagine there was boiler pressure in my jeans trying to break free; when she pressed her body up to mine and gave me a wet kiss on the lips, the pressure spiked and then exploded.

"It's okay." She whispered, leading me into the house and closing the door. "It's my first time too." I didn't tell her the truth. It had been a while since my last encounter, and I was overexcited. Of course, being up close and tortuously personal with her body doubled my excitement.

I leaned the shovel against the stable wall and pulled up my shirt collar trying to hide the hickey Jenna had given me afterwards. I glanced over toward Jase and saw at least five pronounced love bites: he didn't seem to care if the whole world saw.

When my eyes caught Michael's, he just smiled and winked, and then proceeded to hook-up the water bucket in his horse's stall and tossing in a couple of flakes of hay before leaving.

"See you guys later down at Esposito's."

"Later bud." Jase said, giving me a strange look. "Michael seem chirperer to you this morning?"

"Not really," I shrugged.

But Michael did seem possessed of an airy spring step that I hadn't previously noticed. Michael always seemed to be able to meet girls as if by magic—he seemed to flit from one to another like a honeybee searching for nectar, never dating one more than two weeks before moving on to the next. In retrospect, Michael couldn't have bedded all the girls he dated, but I believe he had more than most boys our age. For some reason, he seemed to attract the wayward or boisterous girls in town to his doorstep, which was probably why he never got very serious with any of them outside a quick roll in the hay now and then. Until I saw Michael that day with Caryn, I'd never seen him enthralled with any girl.

I met him at the pizza parlor a little early. Jase, having to do some yardwork at home, said he'd catch up with us around seven. Michael and I sat on the hood of his car and watched the parade of girls and hotrods milling about for another Saturday night in small town America.

"She's my other half," said Michael. "I'll never love another. *Ever.*"

He told me one of his 'odd' feelings came over him late Friday night. "Norwegian Wood" was playing on the radio as Michael described how he'd taken a drive down Sherman Road that led to a cemetery by Sugar Creek. (We often took dates there to drink and fool around.) He parked at the graveyard and reclined on the GTX's hood; while staring at the moon, he'd heard sounds like a struggle coming from the shadows near one of the crypts. "I didn't move for about a minute until I heard this scream and saw what looked like someone running across the graves towards the road," Michael said.

He decided to head them off to see what all the commotion was about. Michael told me that when he'd reached the streetlight near the old Episcopal church, he could see a disheveled girl in a torn dress. He grabbed her and asked what was wrong, already knowing because she was crying and carrying on so.

"Mon chérie! Oh, I'm so glad to see you," she exclaimed. "Hold me. Don't let him hurt me."

"She was speaking in perfect French," Michael told me, "I understood every word. And she seemed to *know* me!" I didn't find this hard to believe because Michael had a perfect memory and studied several languages. As for the knowing part, Michael was one of the school's top athletes, so he was familiar to everyone.

"Yeah," I said, "but you know French, right?"

"Spanish, German, Russian and Chinese, only." I blinked. I did that sometimes. "I just started French." When Michael said these things, I'd feel time stop and myself shift suddenly into a kind of limbo.

He said that while he was trying to get the girl to calm down, Billy Western came out of the shadows, his shirt off and zipping up his pants, with a look on his face like he was ready to kill.

"Leave it alone, Bear! This isn't any of your business!"

Billy Western was a senior who stood six foot three and weighed in at a muscular two-hundred ten pounds. No one, not even the wannabe cowboys who acted so tough out at the barns, dared to take him on in a fight without at least three back-ups, each of them carrying clubs. Even Jase, considered one of the toughest kids in town, who had fought Billy the previous year, didn't dare cross him.

"I blacked out," Michael said when trying to describe the blind rage that came over him when he saw Billy and knew what he'd tried to do to her. "When I came to my senses, my foot was on his neck, and his face was all purple and bloody, and the girl was pulling at my arm saying something in French that I took to mean, 'let's go, let's go .'"

"Billy's a mean one," Jase responded after hearing the story for himself. "Ain't no way I'd fight him again without help."

Michael took her home and she invited him in. In fact, she lived next door to Jenna over on Parcae Avenue, and Michael said he could hear us grunting away because Jenna's bedroom window was open. He claimed he heard her yell out my name, but I didn't believe him because sometimes he intentionally lied to bewilder me. In retrospect, perhaps he could have heard us: Jenna and I were noisy.

Michael continued: "I followed her inside to make sure she'd be okay because on the drive home all she did was cry. Her mother was up waiting, and when she saw me, she gasped and smiled, said something in French, and asked me to have a seat."

He said that while the girl cleaned herself up in the bathroom, her mother started reading his palm.

"Man, you should see her," said Michael who seemed to be reliving the reverie. The album must have been *Rubber Soul* because now Paul McCartney was singing "Michelle." Michael continued: "Striking. I mean, she's beautiful. And her voice is like tinkling crystal. She was wearing this long, black skirt and black silk blouse and had several beaded necklaces around her neck. And her hair, *damn*. Long, black, shining, and she has these big blue eyes that just bore right into you."

"The house was thick with the aromas of roses and violets. She was wearing some perfume that made me feel woozy. I felt like I was under the influence of some kind of hypnotic drug," said Michael. He told me that she kept speaking softly in French as she read his palm and smiled. He felt dizzy. "I was about to pass out when the girl came out of the bathroom. She was drying her hair with a towel, and when she took it away and flipped her hair back our eyes met and my heartbeat was like a horse that had just set a new Derby record. Her mother leaned back, smiled and said to me, Michael this is my daughter Caryn."

We had just flipped the record and were listening to John Lennon sing, "In My Life." I thought we were relaxed and chill, so it rather startled me when Michael impulsively grabbed my arm and said in an intense whisper, "I hadn't *told* her my name."

"Aw heck, Michael," I said with some annoyance, wrestling my arm free. "That ain't so strange. Just about everyone in town knows us."

"Yeah? Well, they just moved to town a couple of days ago. She's not even enrolled in school yet. And it was the way her mother said it, as if, I don't know, she'd been expecting me or something."

Then Michael told me that the girl, Caryn, had come over to him, knelt down, took his hands in hers and said, "My darling, my love. At last we are together."

"*Okay*," I said, understanding (while not excusing) Michael's sudden burst of intensity. "That's a little weird."

"Yeah. Especially since she said everything in French."

He said when he looked into her big round eyes that were like the fluffy sad eyes of a puppy, it felt like he'd known her forever.

"Just wait until you meet her." Michael was indeed smitten. "You'll see. There's something, *magical* about her."

He had that right. The first time I saw Caryn, walking down Jackson Street towards Esposito's, her long bushy brown hair swaying gently in the breeze, wearing a black mid-length cotton dress and tightly fitting black calf boots, I about lost my load. The girl, who I later learned was barely fourteen, already exuded sensuality. She had a round little head, large brown eyes that had an oriental slant, and full doughy lips that inspired dreams of diving into them.

"Holy mother in heaven!" Jase said, whistling at Caryn as she strode up, hugged Michael and placed a long, wet kiss on his mouth. "Where the *hell* did you meet her, bud?"

They made the perfect couple. Partially because they were the same height, but also because it just felt right that they were together. Michael wrapped his arm around her shoulders—Caryn smiled at him like a queen admiring her champion—and said, "You wouldn't believe it, Jase." He turned to me and added, "Would he?"

"I doubt it, man."

It was the perfect year; right up until Caryn turned fifteen. Jase and I were dating Jenna and Tippy regularly every weekend. Michael and Caryn, well, they might as well have been married as much as they were together. In fact, during that entire year they were together, I doubt they spent more than two days apart.

Michael and Jase had met their true loves, but even though I was satisfied with Jenna, my heart still yearned for Caitlyn.

CHAPTER SIX

GHOST RACE

March 1969

JAMES DEAN, the Hollywood star and homegrown Indiana legend, died near Paso Robles, California when his silver Porche Spyder wrecked. The crash happened in 1955, at the intersection of US 466 and CA highway 41. The famous actor is buried at Park Cemetery in Fairmount, near Noble. According to local lore, his silver Porche likewise returned with Dean to Indiana: on dark nights, it is sometimes sighted on State Road 37.

***

Jase was a tinkerer. One of his favorite pastimes was working on cars. He could tear down and rebuild an engine in less time than it took most people to read the manual. By working as a day laborer on weekends, he earned money to support his habit of constantly making adjustments and improvements to the black two-door 1964 Chevelle Super Sport he'd rescued from the Noble Salvage Yard out on Sherman Road about a mile before reaching Sugar Creek Cemetery.

Local contractors were always looking for good helpers, and Jase, being not only dexterous with his hands but a damn hard worker, was always getting jobs doing roofing, dry-walling, and other general labor assignments. Gene Noble, owner of Noble Hardware and the Noble Auto Repair and Customization Shop, often hired Jase as a part-time mechanic.

"By law," Mr. Gene told him on several occasions, "I can't bring you in full time, Jase. However, after you graduate from high school, you'll have a job waiting." Jase, of course, could have dropped out at 16; he didn't need to graduate from high school to work. Gene Noble lied to Jase countless times but did him a higher service.

Just about everyone at school who wanted their cars souped up or given some minor repairs, even things as simple as oil changes, brought them to Jase. In the evenings, over at his house on Francis Street in the Noble Slums, we'd all gather around waiting as Jase either helped someone make adjustments to their car or worked on that damn Chevelle.

Not once did he ask Michael for money.

"Car means more to someone when they pay for it themselves," Jase said one night while our group sat around watching him install a new four-barrel carburetor. We were listening to Jimmy Hendrix sing "Hey Joe" on an old Matsushita transistor radio and wondering when Jase would injure himself. He never did. "My money and my sweat," he continued, "are going to make this car mine."

He slid behind the wheel and turned the key. The engine cranked but didn't fire. Pumping the gas pedal, he turned the key again. Flames two feet high shot out of the carb, a loud bang exploded from the dual exhaust and smoke filled the area. Making a face, Jase stuck his head under the hood saying, "Seems to need just a little adjustment." When he got back behind the wheel and turned the key, the engine roared to life, idling like the panting of a panther ready to strike.

"Easy," Jase said, wiping his greasy hands on a towel and hunkering down beside the car watching with pride as it idled. Though rescued from a junkyard, the Chevelle was only 5 years old; how it became worn down and reduced to salvage was a mystery to us. Michael mused, perhaps half-seriously, that the car was cursed; however, if that were true, Jase was a priestly mechanic casting evil demons from the engine, exorcising unclean spirits away from the distributor cap, and so on.

Tippy and Jase's mother came out the back door carrying tall glasses of iced tea for each of us.

"Finally got that thing running, I see," his mother said, handing Jase his tea. "About time. You been working on it for five months now."

"Just taking my time to do it right." He spat, watching the car as it seemed to jerk and wiggle before settling down again to an easy purr. "Besides, parts ain't cheap."

The Chevelle let out a loud bang and the engine cranked to silence.

"Should have spent your money more wisely on a good used car," his mother said, walking back into the house.

I saw Jase spit again, casting a glance at Michael's GTX parked on the street.

"Someday, I'm gonna have me a really good car."

"Only needs to be broken in, man," Michael said. "It just needs a good hard run on a straight road where you can really open her up. Of course," he added, "I'll have to drive extra slow so you can keep up. Top speed of that thing of yours being only about half that of a slow-moving mule."

Jenna and I set down our glasses and exchanged sighs. Tippy was already moving around the Chevelle to the passenger side, and Caryn was inching backwards towards the curb.

Jase looked at the dull black of his Chevelle, and the bright sparkling metallic green of the GTX, then said with a spit, "Race."

Michael, Caryn, Jenna and I ran to his car and dove inside, just about the time we heard the Chevelle roar to life and the tires churning gravel. Jase had the Chevelle backed down the driveway and, spinning tires, flew past us around the corner of Francis and Crescent heading towards Main before Michael turned his key.

"Damn, he's fast," I said buckling up as Michael fired up the 440 Magnum of the GTX.

"Not to worry," Michael winked at me and smiled. "He has less than a quarter gallon of gas." I was confused, but he said, "Much as he's always bragging, I figured I'd play a little trick on him by draining the tank and moving and locking the fuel gauge to full. I knew once challenged he couldn't resist to show off."

Caryn crossed her arms and gave Michael a stern look. Smiling, he said innocently, "What?"

About halfway down the road to Sugar Creek, we saw Jase pull over to the side. Michael pulled beside him and stopped. "Problems?"

"Yeah, damn it." Jase was more disappointed than angry. "This thing is never going to run. Bucked and spat all the way out here, then just died. I guess Mom was right," he said about as crestfallen as his tough exterior would allow. "It is a piece of junk."

"Might help if you put some gas in it, bud." Michael said, getting out and opening the trunk. "Oh, look here, I just happen to have a couple of gallons."

I was out of the car and pulling Jase off Michael in two beats while Tippy and Jenna laughed. Caryn was tapping her foot and giving Michael a look that said he'd be chewed out in private later.

"Damn it, Michael," said Jase, "I shoulda known you'd do something like this."

"Relax." Michael was casually emptying one of the gas cans into the Chevelle's tank. "We'll top off the tank down at the salvage yard and take a drive up to Bloomington. Plenty of places on Highway 37 to give the old gal a good work out."

Highway 37 ran straight from Noble north about eighty or ninety miles to Indianapolis. The road twisted and turned up and down hills but also had long stretches of straight flat pavement perfect for 'blowing out' a new or refurbished engine. The best time to do a 'blow out' being between midnight and 6 a.m., when the road would be nearly deserted. We could have easily taken any other road, but Michael insisted we take Highway 37.

"There's something I want to check out between Bedford and Bloomington." And that's all he'd tell us.

Besides playing pranks on us poor unsuspecting Hoosiers, Michael was also something of a private investigator of things unknown. Since getting his car in the fall of 1968, he would routinely show up at my door in the middle of the night insisting we go now. Funny thing, since hooking up with Caryn, those midnight excursions were starting to get stranger. "Michael," Jenna said, "do you think it's safe? I mean, Jase just got his car running today. Shouldn't he drive it around town a bit, you know, somewhere close to home, until—"

"What? It's safe." Michael smiled. "Jen, what's to worry about? We'll all be with him. If the car falters, no problem. We'll just get a tow for it in the morning." Michael finished emptying the second gas can into Jase's car. "Oh, Jase, here."

"What is it?"

"A magnet. Just tap it a few times on the gauge and it'll be working properly again."

Michael wasn't a mechanic, but then, with the perfect mind he possessed, he didn't need to be. All he'd have to do is scan a book, and bam, instant knowledge. It also helped that he was good with his hands. Combine that with his love for science, and it wasn't too hard for all of us to figure out that he'd found some unique way to stick the fuel gauge.

If he were to direct his activities to something useful, he might do all right for himself. (If someone didn't kill him first.)

Even though it was a Friday night, the stretch of road Michael had us stop on the side of was completely deserted. With so little for teenagers to do and plenty of graduated Cools too good for adult jobs, drag racing was popular—especially on the weekends. Most people would drive up to the strip in Bean Blossom and race for money, pink slips, and thrills. Others would find deserted back roads to race down. It's a wonder more of them weren't killed.

"Okay, Jase, we need to do this fast."

We were all gathered around the cars, huddling together because the evening air had gotten chillier than normal.

"I'll take Caryn about a mile down the road so she can flag the winner," said Michael. We all felt like characters in *Rebel Without a Cause*. "Tippy and Jenna will stay here. When I get back, Jenna, being that she's an impartial participant here, will get us lined up and started."

Michael was a natural leader. He loved taking charge of a situation but was still open to suggestions from the rest of us. However, that almost never happened. I don't know what it was about Michael, but we all trusted his judgment without question.

"Okay, Mikey, jus' let me give the car a final check before we start."

After dropping Caryn off to mark the finish line, Michael returned and lined the GTX up alongside the Chevelle. A lot of people in Noble were of the opinion that Mopar was superior to Chevy in every way. They'd get in disputatious conversations over what car and engine performed better. Some were of the opinion that the larger the engine's cubic inches the more power it could put out.

Michael's GTX had a powerful 440 Magnum with an Interceptor three-speed automatic and 3.55 gearing, which meant that it was expeditious and fast. Jase's Chevelle had a Chevy 396 and four-on-the-floor manual transmission with stock gearing. Chances were good that he'd blow the engine before he hit third gear attempting to catch the GTX with Michael driving.

"More to driving than mashing the gas, Mikey," Jase said, "If the driver is a wus, then he might as well be driving a Ford."

"Just try to keep up, man. Let me worry about how far behind you will be."

Jase motioned for me to ride with him. "I want an impartial witness to how I'm gonna leave his *GeeTeeEx* in the dust."

Tippy hated when Jase started to brag. He'd already blown the engine in his mom's Impala trying to outrace Michael. Truth of it all, no one could beat Michael in a race. He had this way of pushing the limit. Anyway, it took brass gonads to race those muscle cars. Some, like Michael's, could hit speeds of 150 mph: his gonads were made of Herculean diamonds.

"Racing is not a game for those who play safe," Michael said as he revved his engine, performing a quick burnout that filled the air with putrid smoke. "If you want to win, you've got to take chances. That's what separates us from the weenies who just cruise the lot down to Esposito's."

Jenna stood in the middle of the road waiting. Jase revved his engine, several times, making the Chevelle wiggle, rise and bounce; Michael sat coolly behind the wheel of his car staring directly ahead, the GTX now sitting steady idling quietly.

"Give up, Jase," she said. "Michael's in his special place."

There were times when Michael would zone out. He'd go into a trance and nothing could knock him out of it until he was good and ready. Supposedly, he learned it as part of some martial arts training he'd been involved with for several years. Michael, as we all found out back in December of '68 when he'd knocked Billy Western through the doors of Esposito's, was a seventh-degree black belt in some "secret art" he called it, and said he was under oath not to say more.

"Ready!" Jenna held up her hand. "Go!" When she dropped her hand, all hell broke loose.

Engines roared and tires screamed. I was sure the Chevelle's front end rose up off the ground as both cars shot forward bumper-to-bumper. Jase popped second gear before I knew what was happening and was redlining the engine, keeping perfect pace with Michael.

"Don't blow 'er Jase! Shift already!" The tach was buried, and I heard a loud bang.

"Relax man," Jase assured me, "we just blew the carbon." Then he was in third gear, redlining in seconds, pulling forward of the GTX.

We passed Caryn, who was on the side of the road waving a white t-shirt. Jase slammed fourth, flooring the accelerator. I was pushed back in my seat watching the tach mounted on the top of the dash as it redlined again. By now we'd passed Michael and were leaving him behind.

"Jase," I shouted, "ease up! We won!"

I could see the speedometer needle was completely buried as we continued to accelerate. "JASE!" I heard another loud popping, bang, and saw what I thought were headlights coming towards us. Jase took his foot off the gas pedal and allowed the car to slow as he down shifted to a stop.

Michael's car flew past us like a cannonade of green lightning.

"Lord, Jase!" I shrieked, "he's gonna ram that car coming at us!"

There was a bright flash of light that blinded us momentarily. I expected to hear the earsplitting crash of metal as two cars hit at a combined speed of two hundred miles an hour. But there was only silence. Out of the darkness, I heard the rumble of dual exhaust as the GTX glided to an easy stop beside us.

"Did you guys see it?" Michael asked, as casual and cool as always.

"See what?" We answered. Since we should have been flayed all over the interior of the car, Jase and I must have felt a little perplexed.

"That silver Porche Spyder. It went right past us."

I looked at Jase who just shrugged.

"Honestly, Mikey," said Jase, who did not show his fear easily, "I expected that the three of us would be spread out on the road like butter on hot toast. For sure, I thought you were a goner. What happened?"

"Well, as I passed you, I was slowing and pulled over to the left to do a bootlegger, when I saw it flash past a few inches from the passenger side."

"Saw what? All we saw was a hell of a bright light," I said.

Michael shook his head as if trying to make sense out of nonsense.

"Nothing," he finally said. "Must have been a car passing on the access road or something. Maybe it was just a low-flying chopper. By the way, Jase, nice race. That car of yours is a real roadrunner."

Jase sighed, "I wish I had one of those."

The next day Michael told us that the stretch of road we had been on was rumored to have the ghost of James Dean driving it. Most people who claim to have seen the silver death car say they saw it while racing. I don't know myself. But I do know that whatever made the bright light that blinded us was not a low flying chopper.

CHAPTER SEVEN

WEREWOLF HOLLOW

WEREWOLF HOLLOW has lain quietly beneath its canopy of trees for hundreds, if not thousands, of years. Six hundred acres of dense forest and abandoned quarries contain its secrets. There's a 30-acre lake, called Blood Moon Lake, surrounded by white pine and spruce trees. Bordering the southern edge of the lake and Grey Wolf Hill to the north, there's an endless series of unexplored limestone caves running through the hollow. A single lane dirt road winds its way through the hollow beneath the canopy of trees that keeps it in perpetual twilight. People living in the surrounding hamlets, towns and small cities never venture into what they call the most haunted woods in Indiana. Whenever the Moon rises full above the tree tops, and as it wanes to crescent, doors and windows of the homes near the hollow are shut and barred, and dogs are tied with heavy chains to metal stakes driven deep into the ground inside barns. Blood curdling screams that pierce the otherwise peaceful night and scratching on doors and walls are attributed to the wind blowing through the trees and echoing in the canyons of the forgotten and abandoned quarries. No one living, so stories say, has ever seen what really lives in the hollow, and no one wants to know—except for teenagers with too much time on their hands and a leader who insists on investigating every mystery southern Indiana seems to contain.

"Don't get lost. Very funny. Michael!" I lost Michael as soon as we entered the caves. The darkness bore down around me in such an oppressive manner that I actually became, for lack of a better comparison, sea sick. "Michael!"

As I wound my way through the narrow tunnels that had been cut through the limestone by uncounted ages of flowing water, events of the previous few hours replayed over and over in my weary mind.

"Michael!" I paused. Listened. It seemed as though my friend had pulled aside the veil separating the world of the living from the world of the dead, and stepped through.

Michael J. Bear was obsessed, driven to find answers to mysteries wherever they could be found. His research and obsession with the occult had intensified since hooking up with Caryn back in the fall of 1968. As such he insisted, often at the most inopportune times, that we—our entire group—accompany him on what he called his 'Midnight Excursions.' Even though I've known Michael since kindergarten, I never realized how little he actually slept until that fateful night in August 1969.

"What the..." I stammered, trying to force my eyes open. "Michael? Dang it man, it's one in the morning."

"Get dressed. We have to go. Now!" He urged over the phone. "This cannot wait. Caryn and Jenna are already waiting for us. I'll be there in two minutes."

Two minutes? I thought. It'll take me that long to find the bathroom. But that was Michael for you. Time meant nothing to him, and he often forgot that the rest of us needed to sleep. I barked my toes on the coffee table leg and hopped across the living room in the dark trying not to scream in pain.

We'd been out earlier, drinking beer with Caryn, Jenna, Jase and Tippy down at the Sugar Creek Cemetery and had just got in around eleven. I passed out on the sofa. My parents were gone for the weekend to see the Grand Ole Opry in Tennessee, so I was alone in the house.

Normally, Jenna would have joined me, but she was having some aunt visiting for a few days and said we'd have to wait until the next weekend to fool around. By the time Michael called around one o'clock, I was already deep inside the void of nothingness of my intoxicated stupor. In short, I was out. Usually, I could sleep through anything, and often did when I was drunk. But whenever Michael called, my mind just knew it was him and I'd come awake.

(Well, mostly awake anyway.)

He came bolting through the door and tossed my clothes to me as I stumbled out of the bathroom still caught halfway between being a wakeful soul and a somnambulant wreck.

"Come on," he said pushing me out the door half-naked, "you can dress on the way."

"What the heck is it this time, man?" I was struggling to get my pants on as he revved up the 440 of the GTX and spun tires.

"You'll see," he said, as the car veered around the corner of my street and south onto Grant Street. We spun rapidly through the stop sign where Grant crosses Circle, turned left, and flew around the bend, spun left again over the tracks and took a hard right onto Johnson Avenue.

"Jump in the back. Hurry."

I rolled over the seat into the back as he slowed to ten miles an hour. As we neared Caryn's house, he bent over and threw open the passenger door, and Caryn and Jenna hoped in just in time as he accelerated. Jenna crawled over the seat to join me.

"What the heck is going on this time?" she asked, helping me on with my shirt and shoes.

"How should I know? Didn't Caryn say anything?"

"Nope. She said he called, told her to get me and wait out front."

The car was sliding to a halt at the train depot where Jase and Tippy joined us. Then Michael floored the accelerator and headed down the backstreets towards Sherman Road.

"Mikey," Jase said trying to wake up as he slid over the seat into the back. "What's this all about?"

As soon as Jase put her in the front seat, Tippy placed her head on Caryn's lap and passed out. Tippy lived in one of those three story original Noble homes next to the old train depot, and Jase spent many a weekend night at her house, partly as a way to avoid his father who often came home drunk after spending a night down at Poole's Bar with the other Noble cretins. Unlike us, Jase's dad was a mean drunk who often took pleasure in beating on members of his family. When things got too bad, Jase would go stay with Tippy's family for a few days.

"Can't say," responded Michael. "Just hang loose. We'll be there in 45 minutes."

"Fine," I said, and placed my arm around Jenna, who was leaned back in the seat. "Wake me then." And I passed out.

You ever have one of those dreams where you think you hear something, then wake up and you still hear it? Well, I have and believe me, it isn't fun. I was dreaming that I was walking in the woods late at night. The air was cool and the full Moon hung low in the sky, looking for all the world like a giant ball you could almost reach out and touch. I was feeling pretty good, and just when I thought, *man this is great, I feel so peaceful*, the air split open with the barking howl of a wolf.

The shock startled me so badly that I jumped and hit my head on the roof of the car. As I was shaking my head to push off the drowsiness, I heard it again. If you have never heard that sound before, don't go trying to find it. Trust me. You don't want to. Every hair on my body stood on end and my eyes flew open so wide I thought my eyeballs were going to pop out. The third howl made my blood freeze.

"What the heck was that?" No one could hear me. They were all standing out in front of the car in the beams of the headlights listening. A fourth howl rang out as I strode up to my group of friends.

"Wolves?" I stammered.

"Not quite, bud."

"Sounds like wolves to me," Jase said, holding Tippy a little too tightly I noticed.

"Nope. Wolves don't howl...like this." Michael was standing with his hands on his hips, Caryn, in her black dress and boots, stood beside him. Their long hair, his black and hers brown, whipped about gently in the early false dawn morning breeze. Michael was also wearing his usual adventuring clothes: black sneakers, black jeans and black t-shirt. They looked like a witch and warlock ready to do battle with forces unseen. And knowing their spirits, they'd give a pretty damn good accounting of themselves if they did.

Jenna backed up and I wrapped my arms around her. She was shaking like a willow in a typhoon.

"Werewolves," Caryn said, in a matter-of-fact tone that sent chills up my spine.

You know, as much as I liked Caryn, sometimes she was a little eerie. Michael wasn't spooky, just weird. Okay, Michael could be spooky too, but neither was as spooky as Caryn's mother, who earned money—usually on the weekends in her spare time —working as a fortune teller. Cassandra, Caryn's mother, is a real gypsy. Not the kind you read about in books or see misportrayed in movies, like that one with Lon Chaney, but an actual Romanian Gypsy (with some French acculturation to boot). How she and Caryn ended up in small town America is a story unto itself.

Anyway, Cassandra had this way of looking at you that gave you the willies, but not in a bad way. Her penetrating azure eyes, staring out of her round face surrounded by mounds of raven locks, tended to see into your soul, while her beauty set you at ease. She always wore these flowing skirts, usually black, loose silk or cotton blouses—mostly black—and necklaces crafted from silver and gold. On her fingers she wore five rings. Exactly five; always the same five. One had an opal, one a ruby, one an emerald, one a sapphire and one, I kid you not, was a solid band of platinum that had weird carvings engraved all over it. And her jewels weren't no small quarter-carat rip-offs you can buy at the mall jewelry store in Bloomington; they were big and real. Precious cuts, she called them.

The first time I met her, she smiled, nodded, invited us in for tea— an oddly sweet mixture that had the ability to make you feel relaxed— called Jase and me by name (nobody had told her our names as yet) and made reference to something called a *triumvirate*, or some such.

"You are three who make one," she said, in her soft eastern European French-like tone.

Jase and I thought she was a bit weird; doubly so when she reached into a box that seemed to appear out of nowhere. The thing contained all kinds of items—rings, pins, roughcut precious stones, I saw a lot of something she called onyx, and necklaces. She handed me a little silver band ring saying, "Caitlyn says hello." The ring was engraved with the words *Find Me*, with Caitlyn's name on the inside. Caitlyn had been my first love, but had disappeared the winter of seventh grade.

I've never taken the ring off since that day Cassandra gave it to me. Somehow, I thought it might lead me back to Caitlyn.

"Werewolves?" We all said in unison.

Three more piercing howls sounded in succession sending more chills racing though my body.

Michael turned around and said quite seriously: "Werewolves."

I would have told Michael to stop pulling my leg, if it wasn't for all the howling that kept ringing through the trees. Michael enjoyed making us the butt of his jokes, usually after a very prolonged and, sometimes, rather involved series of riddles, mysteries and disinformation. Once he was sure that Jase and I were completely under his spell, he'd pop the punch line. However, from the look on his face, and Caryn's, something told me that this time he was deadly serious.

They each wore these identical silver medallions—a triangular figure made of three arcs interwoven within a circle; his had a ruby in the center and hers had an opal—on short silver necklaces. Cassandra had given them to Michael and Caryn the day she gave me Caitlyn's ring, saying to them: "Bound in spirit, bound in love, eternally."

I looked at their medallions and got one of those feelings. Sometimes I worried about those two.

Jase, however, felt a slight tugging on the cuff of his pants.

"Aw, hell, Mikey, dang it. I ain't got time for these games of yours after drinking all night and not getting any rest."

More howls assaulted our ears. Jenna wrapped her arms around my neck so tight I thought my head was going to pop off. I swear, if she could have at that moment, she would have crawled right up into my shirt pocket and hid.

"Let's get out of here!" she said.

Tippy was already in the car hiding in the backseat on the floorboard with her arms clutched tightly over her head.

"Relax. They're moving away from us. Michael," Caryn was all business now. "We better get moving." I reckon she felt at home among the dark forest and the wolves—at least I'd heard Romania and France had lots of wolves.

"Okay. Everyone to your usual positions. Let's roll!"

Our usual positions meant that Caryn would be up front next to Michael, Jase in the back behind the driver's seat, next to him Tippy, with Jenna behind the front passenger seat, where I sat riding shotgun. The only difference this time being, Michael actually handed Jase and me short-barrel shotguns, which he called *greeners*, that he'd quickly removed from the trunk.

"Take these." He handed each of us a box containing 12-gauge deer shells, but with silver slugs. He then strapped on an official western-style gun belt and rolled the cylinder of his Colt revolver checking its loads. "And don't shoot unless you have to."

We were all well acquainted with firearms. Dad taught us to shoot when we were six. We'd walk down to the pond on Uncle John's farm up near Franklin, and shoot frogs with a .22 caliber rifle. Mom bought the rifle for Dad back in 1943, so he could track down and kill a black panther that had been seen bothering livestock on their farm where Monroe Reservoir is now. Sometimes I shudder thinking about what secrets are buried beneath all that water; just like I was shuddering as Michael drove us down the little hill that took us deep into the hollow.

"What exac' are we looking for, Mikey?" Jase asked, scanning the tree line. "You're not really serious about this werewolf thing, are you?"

"I am." And that was all Michael said as the GTX crept along at an easy 20 miles an hour.

Now I was feeling my pants' leg being tugged and told Michael to stop the car.

"What?!" he asked a little perturbed.

Did I also mention, at any time, that Michael's parents are rich? How wealthy they are, I can't say, but Michael had access to money. Lots of it. I began to think about just how wealthy Michael was, and decided that if he wanted to pull an elaborate joke like this, he definitely had the resources to do it. However, before I could confront him about what poor taste such a joke was in, something happened that made us all believers.

"Okay Micha—" The foliage to my right began to shake violently and this—thing—jumped out and into the road directly in front of the car. The creature was over six feet tall, covered in greyish brown hair, with these great big jaws that contained what looked like the nastiest, sharpest teeth I've ever seen on any animal.

My hair must have been standing on end because I could feel the fabric covering the inside of the car's roof. The thing opened its mouth wide, about a half-gallon of saliva dripping onto the ground, and howled.

Michael and Caryn seemed to be smiling.

"Okay, okay, I believe you! I believe you! Now what?"

"Now," Michael said casually, "we see if it's real or not."

He stepped out of the car and walked around to the front with Caryn at his side. I was on the passenger side of the car with a shotgun ready to blast the thing away, only I was too afraid to actually do it. The monster's eyes wavered back and forth between us. It stepped forward three steps and stopped. The thing had its teeth bared and was growling menacingly, and I could smell a putrid mustiness emanating off the beast that told me it was definitely not human. Michael eased his revolver out of its holster, the beast just standing there in the headlights, growling, snarling, but not moving, except those red eyes. I swear I thought I saw it raise an eyebrow as it glowered at me.

I heard the hammer on the revolver clicking back to fully cocked. The floorboard of the backseat now contained three very scared teenagers, and I heard Caryn whisper something in French. I guessed she'd never seen a wolf like the one standing in front of the car before. Just when I expected to hear the bang of Michael's gun, another howl rang out, this time from what appeared to be quite a ways off. The beast suddenly dropped to all fours and disappeared down the road.

"Damn it," Michael said, motioning Caryn inside before jumping back behind the wheel and flooring the accelerator. I was barely in my seat as the car sped off.

"Michael," I asked tremulously, "what did you mean by seeing if it was *real?*"

"After I dropped you all off earlier, I went home and did some reading. In a book about mysteries of Indiana, I came across a story about a place the locals call Werewolf Hollow."

The car was bouncing down the road at an even 50 miles an hour. The road turned and twisted like a maddening version of a pretzel.

"I thought it was a bunch of bunk, but wanted to check it out anyway. I figured we had enough time to reach the place, after checking its location on one of my maps, just before full Moon set, and just might be able to... well, you heard the howls."

In fact, I was still hearing them over the roar of the duel exhaust of the GTX's powerful engine.

"And prove what, exactly?" I asked running my eyes along the tree line and front of the car.

"I want to find out whether or not a legend about a tribe of wild people still living in the hollow is either true or false. People who think they are wolves."

Okay, now he was getting really spooky.

"Werewolves are real, my love." Caryn was getting spookier as well. "Mother told me so."

Jase was peeking over the back of the seat.

"Real or not, must we go about chasing them?" He was obviously more scared than I'd ever seen him. And Jase didn't scare easily. He told us about this one time when he was visiting some relatives down near Nancy, Kentucky, where he'd had a run in with some ghosts. Naturally, we didn't believe him. Michael figured everything had a rational explanation; I just wasn't sure either way.

After everything we'd been through up to that point, I was still a sceptic wanting to believe.

Whether that thing we'd seen was werewolf, man-wolf, or just a really big wolf, gave me enough reason to want to get out of that place of oppressive darkness.

"Relax, man. Just have that shotgun ready," Michael said a bit too casually. "We're almost there."

What? I thought. Almost where?

As if reading my thoughts, Michael smiled and said, "The lair."

Tippy and Jenna were still on the floorboard.

"Are you crazy?" Jase and I said together.

Michael's smart, real smart, in fact he was the smartest kid in our class. Some people said he was the smartest kid in Indiana. But sometimes, when a person is that intelligent, they are a very short step from being outright insane. At the moment, I was sure he'd gone over the edge.

As we rounded a bend in the road, the headlights fell upon the pale limestone backing of an abandoned and drained quarry. The stone walls, cut into a half-circle, looked to be over 200 feet high, and I hoped Michael didn't plan on expecting any of us to climb up those steep, dangerous cliffs.

Indiana is replete with limestone quarries, many of which have been abandoned. I've seen some. They all have large pools of immensely deep water and contain catfish that grow to six feet...so some of the old folks claim. The quarry Michael stopped the car at was bone dry. I figured it had been abandoned for about a hundred years, if not more.

As we got out of the car, Michael said: "There should be a cave down at the bottom somewhere."

Then he turned to Jase: "Stay here with the girls while we check it out."

"Not a problem, man, just leave me the keys."

Michael pulled two flashlights out of the trunk and tossed one to me as he headed across the rocks and down the slope. Jenna gave me a kiss, saying be careful, then I trotted away to catch up with Michael.

The slope descended for at least 600 feet. We slipped and slid and half-jumped from stone to stone and across gravel until we reached the bottom. We found ourselves in a hole about 800 feet wide. Michael found a trail, of all things, and trotted off.

Eventually we came to an opening in the rock face.

"Okay," Michael said, flipping on his light, "try not to get lost. That story I read mentioned that these caves are tricky and have lots of branches."

"Fine," I said, following him inside. Once inside, I lost him almost instantly, as if we'd entered separate realities.

Try not to get lost, I thought, as I flashed the beam of my light around looking for Michael, and trying to catch some sound that would tip me off to his position. The path we were on inside the cave was loose-packed dirt, and I could see tracks covering the surface. The deeper into the caverns I walked, the more they smelled like a crypt. I surmised that Michael must have headed down the trail at a trot because I lost him so quickly, but I still could not shake the feeling that he and I no longer shared the same dimension.

"Just pull aside the veil and step into another world," Michael would sometimes say as we sat out at the Sugar Creek cemetery drinking and talking about philosophy and alternate dimensions.

I just wanted to get out of those labyrinthine caverns, wondering why I'd let him lead me into them in the first place. Sometimes, on our excursions, I wondered if Michael didn't have some secret agenda. I banged my head on a low part of the ceiling and winced.

"Michael!" My voice reverberated through the caves. I moved along turning down various passages, barely able to see two feet in front of me. "Dang it!"

I had been trying for quite some time to find my way back to the opening without success. If there hadn't been so many tracks in the dirt, I might have been able to do so, but every turn looked the same. "MICHAEL!"

Yeah, I was scared, but I wasn't about to let him try to confront whatever it had been that we'd seen alone. I turned down a new tunnel and stopped.

Sitting near a small fire before me was an old man. A really old man. The fire cast enough light for me to see him clearly. His face was brown and leathery, and wrinkled like an old handkerchief that had been wadded up and stuffed into a pocket for several years. But his body, which was covered with nothing besides a loincloth, looked strong. His muscles looked hard and well-defined, not like a body builder, but more like someone who'd spent years in back-breaking manual labor. Kind of like my father who'd spent many years unloading cinder blocks by hand. There were also a lot of drawings on his skin, all in some red pigment that I swear looked like blood. His long, grey hair was secured with a leather headband. And his black eyes—I am telling you the truth here—sparkled, and should have given me the willies, but instead made me feel calm.

He said something I didn't understand, and indicated for me to sit. As I sat, he threw something on the fire that made the flames turn white and scream up to the ceiling, while he chanted. The chant was low, slow, melodic and repetitive, and brought intriguing images to my mind; it felt almost as though the images floating through my tired mind were…memories.

I was sitting with the shotgun resting on my knees, my finger on the trigger, ready to blast the man away if he tried something. But he didn't do anything for a long time besides chant while tossing some white powder into the fire. Yet, strangely enough, I didn't feel any fear. I was actually becoming relaxed and forgot all about what I was doing there.

After a time he looked at me, smiled—he had weird teeth: long, white and sharp—and he said in broken English: "The spirits, uneasy today. Strangers come. Yet, not strangers."

Okay, that sort of talk gave me the willies.

Then he took off the necklace he was wearing and handed it to me. It was a talisman. I knew what such things were because Cassandra had shown us a lot of them. Hanging on a leather string was a small smooth piece of finely polished limestone. Etched into the surface was a strange symbol I didn't at the time know, nor have I ever discovered what it means. If grandmother hadn't died when I was younger, maybe she could have told me.

"You are brother to wolf. No harm come to you in this place."

I tied the talisman around my neck and hid it inside my undershirt. I'm one-fourth Sioux Indian. My mother's grandmother, whose Sioux name translated as White Wolf Who Walks Alone, was one of the Lakota Sioux who survived the massacre at Wounded Knee and came to Indiana shortly thereafter. Her daughter, who was called Little Wolf Who Walks By Night by her tribe, married a young man of Irish descent who worked at the Mather Quarry near Bloomington. I reckoned the old guy sitting before me sensed my bloodline. Maybe that was what he'd meant by stranger, but not stranger.

"You must now go." He said, softly. "Take path to right. You find exit soon."

As I stood to do as he instructed (for some reason I trusted the guy), he added: "They who dwell in this place wish to remain unknown. Although they will not harm brother to wolf, you must keep secret."

I headed off down the tunnel indicated and soon found myself out in the semi-gloom of the hollow. A second later, Michael joined me.

We looked briefly into each other's eyes. Neither of us spoke, but I saw an unusual sparkle in my friend's eyes that told me he too had encountered something strange in the caverns. Then Michael trotted off towards a winding path that led straight to the top.

We drove home in silence. Jase and the girls kept asking us what had happened, but neither Michael nor I said anything. Caryn sat passively beside Michael holding his hand tightly the entire way.

A few days later, Jenna and I were fooling around and she asked me what the talisman was, holding it gently between finger and thumb.

I told her to forget about it and she instantly, seeing the look in my eyes, said, "okay."

None of us ever discussed that outing again. I drove out there a few times trying to find Werewolf Hollow, but was never able to find the road leading down to it. It seemed as if the forest had literally closed up, sealing it from the outside world.

After our trip though, Michael started calling me Brother Wolf.

NOTE

First published in Mallorn *52 in the Autumn 2011 volume. (Courtesy of the Tolkien Society, UK)*

CHAPTER EIGHT

CROSSING SHADOW'S VEIL

September 1969

LUCKY balked refusing to enter the fog covering the trail and blocking out the moonlight. She appeared like a shadow from the mist, transparent in her white dress, before solidifying into the shape of an ageless seductress floating rather than walking towards us. Her long white hair blew wildly on a windless breeze, and her eyes, shimmering like a kaleidoscope, held me transfixed in a wondrous awe of desire. Lucky lowered his head allowing the woman to caress his face with slim brown fingers. No longer afraid, Lucky moved forward as the woman floated backwards, beckoning us, towards the fog.

* * *

It was a night of the full moon. In the background, Jackson C. Frank faintly sang "My Name is Carnival," "Don't Look Back," and "Blues Run the Game" over our well-used transistor radio; the AM station played a few of Frank's songs that night, and his melancholy words blended well with those early autumn noises of soft winds, songs of owls, and crunchy sounds made by small animals crossing our leafy campsite. In the midst of all this, Tava told us another story of the secrets the woods of Brown County held.

The adults were out on a moonlight ride while Michael, Jase, and I remained in camp with our girlfriends eating chili and listening to Michael's grandmother speak of ghosts, wolves, and fairy mounds. I was only half-listening though. My thoughts were elsewhere.

The full moon, big and white shining above the treetops, was beckoning me. A few months before, on a night like this, our group had driven to Werewolf Hollow seeking signs of werewolves. After that night, whenever the moon was full, I felt it tugging at me, luring me into the shadows. My girlfriend, Jenna, was afraid of the night, especially whenever the moon was full. In fact, she refused to be alone with me at these times. She said I was *different* and that difference made her fear me. Tava's stories weren't helping matters.

"He's getting that look again, Mikey." Jase was joking, but I could sense what Michael and Caryn were thinking. They sat holding each other, the campfire between us, as the white flames flickered off their twin silver triquetra pendants. Jenna was sitting with Jase and Tippy eyeing me with concern.

"I can see the hair on his face starting to grow...."

"Stop it, Jase." Michael's words were level but firm. "The joke's getting old."

Our eyes met and we shared the knowing look we had in common after leaving the caves in the hollow. Contrary to Jase's jibes, I never grew hair or ran on all fours howling after the moon; however, my mood would often darken and I could never sleep during the moon's full cycle. Michael said I had itchy feet because I felt the need to roam, usually alone. The higher the moon rose, the more anxious I became to be out on a trail. What I never told my friends was the real reason I took to roaming: I was looking for the veiled entrance into the hollow, the real hollow, where shapeshifters lived hidden from the prejudices of the modern world.

Tava was talking about such places hidden deep in the woods of Brown County.

"Hunters sometimes stumble across barriers of fog that transport them to another dimension." When Tava spoke, I was never sure if she were ruminating on things she knew, or just related to us information she'd come across in Time-Life. Still, she sounded credible. "Sometimes they come back with no recollection of the experience; others never come back at all...."

"Enough!" declared Jenna; she was on her feet walking rapidly towards the girls' tent. "I'm going to bed, and don't even think of bothering me until sunrise."

I had no intentions of spending private time with Jenna that weekend. This was a time for exploring. The sky was clear with a billion stars covering the velvet blackness. The light of the moon created a kind of false dawn that illuminated the trails of the deep woods. Over the years, my friends and I had ridden many a trail on nights like this. However, on this night, I wanted to ride alone. Tava's stories didn't bother me. My friends and I had heard eerier tales from Dad as we rode the trails or rested around a campfire. We knew the stories were just folk tales meant to scare kids in order to keep them from wandering off into the woods alone.

Then Tava began telling a story that was all too familiar to me. A story detailing a personal experience I had never shared with my friends, or anyone else.

"Billy was out hunting one night with his friends when he was cut off from them by an unnaturally thick fog that appeared out of nowhere. After wandering around for hours, unable to find his way back to camp, he suddenly saw a strange yellow light cutting through the mist. The light led him to a small cabin occupied by a lone young woman who fed him and offered her bed for the night. In the morning he awoke lying on a pile of leaves. The woman and the cabin were gone, so he figured the experience had been nothing more than a dream of his weary mind." Tava looked at me with a tiny smile on her withered lips. "Dreams are just fantasies of reality. One must not let himself prefer the dream in favor of living."

That's my story grandma, not my Dad's.

Tava smiled, as if she could read my thoughts, and said, "One lives in the now; one lives in his mind; the third refuses truth his eyes reveal." She let out a low cackle before lighting her pipe, blowing out a long stream of gray smoke while eyeing us all with youthful old eyes. Several loud pops sent embers from the fire into the air and Caryn crossed herself as Tippy gasped.

Midnight was approaching and I was eager to get going. I turned off Jackson Frank so I could bring the radio. As we prepared our horses for the ride, Caryn filled the dark September silence with pleas for Michael to stay, and Tippy implored Jase to keep us safe. Although I wanted to go alone, my friends insisted that wasn't going to happen.

"Our dads will be pissed if we let you go alone this late." Jase said as he swung into the saddle. "Besides, it's a good night for adventure."

We set off at a slow canter single file towards Story. The moonbeams sliced through the trees shielding us in a silvery glow. Our eyes quickly adjusted to the semi-darkness and we were able to see well enough not to need flashlights or cigars. Silence surrounded us except for the pounding of the horses' hooves on the hard-packed dirt trail.

After a while we slowed the horses to a walk and I flipped on the transistor radio. Normally, reception in the woods was intermittent, but on this night the signal came in extraordinarily crystal clear and strong. Instead of more Frank songs, a youthful voice of a female disc-jockey filled the night.

"Welcome fellow travelers of the midnight shadow. I'm Cloe, your late-night hostess with you until dawn on WFTE in Noble. Our next selection comes to you from Jim Morrison and the Doors. *Break on through to the other side....*"

"Must be a new station," Jase said trotting up next to me.

"Who cares?" Michael replied, "As long as the signal is good."

I felt a shiver run through me when the DJ spoke; her voice seemed oddly familiar. I shrugged off the feeling and rode in silence as the music played.

Some people said the music of the Doors was magical, like the conjuring of sorcerers able to open doors into other dimensions, other worlds. I don't know about that. Jase would say hogwash; Michael would insist on proof; I wanted to believe. When the song ended, we saw a mysterious wall-of-fog appear on the trail ahead.

* * *

As I entered the fog, I glanced back and saw that Jase and Michael on their horses seemed frozen in time. A moment later the clicking of Lucky's metal shoes on asphalt made me rein him to a stop. Static screeched from the radio, so I switched it off. The noonday sun shone down on me. I was on a two-lane country road surrounded by forest on both sides. The road stretched forward and behind into infinity, or so it seemed. I nudged Lucky forward and rode in silence until I saw a woman, who appeared to be somewhere between eighteen and twenty-five, standing on the side of the road hitchhiking.

The woman was tall, well-tanned and toned with waist-length straight raven black hair. Her clothing was stylish business attire—black mid-thigh skirt and white long-sleeved silk blouse partially unbuttoned—except for her clear stiletto sandals, that gave her the appearance of an exotic dancer waiting her turn on stage. Silver-rimmed '60s styled mirrored sunglasses covered her eyes, but I knew she was staring directly into my soul; around her neck hung a silver Celtic Trinity symbol representing the Power of Three. As I drew near, she smiled, a bit tensely I thought, and said, "Hello, I am Morrigan."

Two ravens suddenly flew overhead, squawking loudly before

disappearing into the forest. Morrigan placed her left hand on her hip and bent her knee standing a little more casually.

"Don't mind them," she said as she waved her right hand in a dismissive gesture. "They'll get over it."

"What?" I stammered, confused. It wasn't a question in response to her statement as much as bewilderment. The woman's name meant something to me; something Michael had mentioned during one of our philosophical talks out at the Sugar Creek cemetery. Try as I might, I could not recall the information I needed. My mind felt blocked. Like Jase had said, it was a good time for adventure, so I decided to just go with the situation.

"They don't approve of my talking with you." She shook her head and laughed heartily. "Silly birds." Then her demeanor changed, and she became more serious. "Now, whatever shall I do with you, I wonder?" From the look on her face and the way her tongue innocently wetted the black lipstick covering her full lips, I had a feeling she already knew.

She held out her left hand and wiggled her fingers at me. "Come with me."

When I didn't move, she became more insistent. "Come on now, shyness isn't becoming. And don't worry about your horse, he will be all right where he is, plenty of grass to graze on."

I dismounted and took her hand. She led me into the forest to a clearing where stood a small cabin. The only furniture inside the cabin was an oaken four-poster bed with black velvet drapes.

Must be a dream, I thought quickly, rationalizing events.

Morrigan took me in an embrace and kissed my mouth softly, whispering, "If you wish."

Yup, has to be a dream. *I fell off my horse, hit my head and now I'm dreaming.*

"Dream, reality, what's the difference?" Her soft lips kissed my neck as she spoke.

The room was suddenly full of the sweet smell of honeysuckle. We moved as one in an embrace that caused the cabin to swirl as we fell onto the bed. When I looked into her eyes, I saw Caitlyn. Not Caitlyn as I had known her, but an older version, a mature version as she might appear in her mid-twenties. Our lips touched gently, and I felt a surge of wonder and satisfaction rush through me. We held each other tightly, our hands moving slowly and deftly removing and dropping our clothes piece by piece onto the floor.

We merged, joining our bodies, minds, and souls.

I felt at peace.

Afterwards, I walked with Caitlyn/Morrigan in silence back to the road. The sun still sat at its apex although I knew several hours must have passed. At the road we embraced. I kissed her lips not wanting the dream, alternate reality, or whatever this was to end. As I swung into the saddle, I saw a raven fly off. I sat on Lucky, alone on the road, and looked at the ring I constantly wore on my pinky, at the words *Find Me* etched on its surface. Turning Lucky back the way we'd come, I suddenly became dizzy.

* * *

"Whoa there, Bud!" Jase caught me by the arm before I fell out of the saddle. "You okay?"

"I don't know. What happened?"

"Beats me," Michael said, "Lucky just up and spun around and you passed out for a moment."

A moment? I thought, shaking my head to clear up the fog. *Time distortion.* Michael and I had read a number of books about entities referred to as Men in Black who could stretch a single second into several hours, a common occurrence in alien abductions. A better explanation was a waking dream. I had those sometimes back in Noble. One moment I would be wide awake then aware of experiencing an elaborate dream that felt real, only to find out that I had been asleep for just five or ten minutes.

I weighed the evidence: the full moon, Tava's stories, being overtired from lack of sleep, my obsessive hope of finding Caitlyn. In the few seconds that I was out and before Jase had caught me, my mind had taken me on a trip that most pot smoking, acid dropping hippies would pay good money to experience.

Just as I had convinced myself that my experience had been a dream after all, Jase said, "You guys smell honeysuckle?

THIRD PHASE

GEMS IRREGULAR

CHAPTER NINE

Halloween 1969

EVERY day after school we'd take Michael's car, drive down to the train depot and pick up Caryn before heading out to the barns to give the horses their evening feeding. She attended the Catholic school that was about a half mile from her house on Parcae Avenue. The public high school we attended was a mile in the opposite direction. About the time we got to the depot she'd be there waiting. But on Halloween 1969, Caryn's birthday, she was late.

It was an unusual day. An unseasonably thick fog filled the air. In fact, it was so thick that you had to literally push it out of your way to see your own hand. Jase joked on the drive down to the depot that it felt like we were inside a cotton ball. Okay, maybe not that thick, but it was bad. Michael was pacing the tracks looking worried. In fact, he'd been that way all day. He was moody, introspective, as if something was weighing heavily on his mind. Thursday night he'd given Caryn an early birthday present: a silver engagement ring! Michael's parents and Caryn's mother were supportive of them getting married, though they had tacit concerns because both were young for such a commitment. Still, their families seemed approving. Some of us guessed that Caryn was pregnant, but Michael wasn't saying. Parents sometimes sent daughters away from town when they got caught in the family way. Teen pregnancy and drug abuse were taboo subjects in those days; if we needed to know, Michael would tell us in his own time.

"What's up?" I asked. "Relax, she'll be here. Maybe she had to stay after for something."

Michael looked at Jase and me, worry covering his face. He was sweating even though the day was cool.

"Damn guys, I don't know. Maybe I should wait until Caryn gets here, but I don't know, I *feel*...funny."

"Vujaday," Jase chided.

Michael was always having feelings like he'd done something or been someplace before. He said he couldn't escape feelings of *déjà vu* every now and then. Jase liked to make fun of him by saying it backwards. Usually, Michael would laugh and shrug the feelings off, but on this day he didn't laugh. He didn't even smile. Instead, when Jase said, "Vujaday," Michael spun around rapidly and started running down the tracks yelling Caryn's name. What happened next has replayed in my mind like a nightmare ever since.

I saw Michael starting to run down the tracks screaming something to Caryn. Then, through the fog, I saw a bright light that for a brief moment shone on the form of someone walking on the tracks towards the depot. Michael jumped to the side as the bark of an air horn cut through the mist. I felt something wet and warm splash across me, as something heavy slammed into my chest knocking me to the ground. The train roared on past us. I doubt the engineer even realized what had happened.

When the train had passed, I heard the earsplitting screams of a woman.

The fog began to dissipate. Jase was standing by Michael's car, covered in blood and staring straight ahead. Caryn's mother, I often wonder how she could have known, was wailing and running towards us. I was sitting on the gravel looking at a bloody arm laying at my feet. I felt my face, looked at my hand, and saw blood.

Getting shakily to my feet, I dogtrotted down the tracks towards Michael and Caryn's mother. Michael was on his knees, tears flooding his face and mumbling, "My darling, our child...." Caryn's mother, pulling at her hair, spun in circles screaming, her eyes wide as saucers, blind streaking terror etched into her face. I stood frozen as if time had suddenly stopped.

I blinked.

Jenna was hugging Michael and trying to get him to move off the tracks. Tippy and Jase were lachrymose beside the car; it was the first time I ever saw Jase cry. Caryn's mother, standing next to a city police car and holding something in her arms, continued to scream.

In a daze, I walked home, showered, climbed into bed and fell into a deep, terror-filled sleep.

The next day—to the sounds of distant windchimes, with the windows remonstrating gently against the moaning breezes and soft murmuration of mid-autumn leaves outside—Jenna filled me in on what happened that night.

"I took Michael back to Caryn's house. He was still in shock and just kept mumbling to himself. Caryn's mother was in her room, sedated. I felt like someone needed to stay with them. Jase and Tippy, I don't know where they went. After a while, I don't know, two or three hours, I took Michael into Caryn's room and we lay on her bed."

Jenna stopped. Her loose hair fell forward for a minute, and I saw her hands were pressed together. However, I knew she would eventually toss her tresses from her forehead and continue.

"He was trembling," she went on, "all through his body. I didn't know what to do. So, I just held him as tight as I could. Later, like I said, it just kind of happened, we kissed." Jenna said it sadly, but not regretfully.

"After the kissing started, our clothes came off. Once inside me, Michael was like a wild man," said Jenna, reliving for a moment the fear that for her was inseparable from the comfort and pleasure she had shared. "At times, I felt like he was trying to crawl up inside of me. When it finally ended, we were both so exhausted we passed out."

I thought Jenna was finished because she was silent for awhile. Then she said, "When I woke in the morning, Michael was gone. I don't think he knew it was me because he kept calling out Caryn's name the entire time."

The windows seemed to cease their moaning, but I knew there was still wind: I could still hear the distant chimes as Jenna added, "Perhaps he didn't see me. I think he only saw her."

I should have been angry, but instead I hugged Jenna and told her it was okay. After what had happened to Caryn, how could I be angry? After all, Michael was my friend. My brother.

A month passed before I saw Michael again. He was wearing a silver ring on his left pinky. I recognized it as the ring he had given Caryn for her fifteenth birthday. The words *True Love* were etched into the surface joined by the infinity symbol with their names etched on the inside.

"It's all I have left of her." Michael said, with the barest hint of a smile.

I never saw him smile or laugh again.

CHAPTER TEN

December 1969

MICHAEL sold me the GTX for five hundred dollars about a week after Caryn died, claiming it held too many memories.

"I can't get her smell out of the car," he said. "No matter what I do, I keep smelling roses and violets all the time."

I didn't know what he was talking about; neither did Jase because we didn't smell anything. *What the hell*, I thought, *I'll take care of it and when he decides he wants it back, I'll give it to him.* Jase and I both knew what the car meant to Michael, and what it had come to represent. Somehow, seeing him driving the thing without Caryn sitting beside him wasn't natural.

Michael's father, feeling bad about Caryn's death and knowing how his son felt about losing their newly created child as well, bought him a black 1956 T-Bird for Christmas.

"I know it won't fill up the void, son," he said. Michael's father said the Thunderbird was an ancient Native American symbol for strength, power, and freedom. In his own way, he was trying to tell Michael something that would take him years to comprehend.

The T-Bird had bucket seats with a console between them. He would never again own a car that would allow a female passenger to sit butted up against him.

"I appreciate the gesture, dad."

Déjà vu.

Michael told us that he was getting another one of his feelings. This time, Jase kept his mouth shut.

"Come on, man," he said, slipping behind the wheel of the 1968 Roadrunner he'd just bought, "let's see what she's made of."

I don't know how we ever survived. After Caryn died, Michael was like a man possessed. He pushed everything to the ultimate limit. That night was a clear and warm evening—'false-summer' we called it. We were out looking for something to do and found ourselves on Carrion Road, a twisting, curving road that had a two-mile stretch of hard dangerous curves.

"No one has even been able to drive this stretch faster than forty-five miles an hour," Jase said. Instantly, I wish he hadn't said anything.

"I'll do it at sixty," Michael said.

"Can't be done," I advised, seeing that he was hellbent on trying.

"Someone go with him," Jenna said, making a solicitous face that sent chills of jealousy through my blood. After she told me, I thought I was beyond such 'bourgeois sentiments,' but, in the weeks and months that followed, what Jenna told me about her and Michael created more strain despite the circumstances. I brushed the thought away.

We were all together—me and Jenna in the GTX, Jase and Tippy in his Roadrunner, and Michael in the T-Bird.

"Jase," Tippy warned, "I swear if you let him do it alone, I'll walk home." She pushed him towards Michael's car as he revved the engine. Jase, often so cocksure, seemed to hesitate.

"No way," he said. "If Mikey has a death wish, then let him go ahead and do it."

Before I knew what was happening, Jenna was sliding into the passenger seat of the T-Bird and yelling over her shoulder, "You all keep up. I'll make sure he doesn't do anything stupid."

"Damn it!" I spat, jumping into my car as Michael spun gravel. Now it was on. "Jase! Let's go!"

I don't know how he did it. Jase and I were fighting hard as hell to stay on the road, our speedometers pegging fifty, but Michael just lost us. At the midway point is a short stretch of straight road. There I pulled my car over and Jase stopped behind me.

"Damn him!" I yelled to Jase, "If he hasn't gone completely over the edge."

"Where'd they go?" Jase and I were out of our cars scanning the darkness.

"Hell if I know! There's nowhere to go!"

In the distance, we heard the whine of an engine and tires screaming on pavement.

"Damn it, Jase, he's coming back, and it sounds like he's high-balling her!"

Suddenly, we saw headlights bending around the corner and heard tires screaming like they were about to blow.

"He's crazier than a shithouse rat! Look out!"

Leave it to Michael to find the only hump in a flat road. We watched in horror as the T-Bird got airborne and flew straight for a large oak tree near the side of the road. Michael was either the luckiest son of a bitch in the world or he had a guardian angel. Whatever the case, instead of the car wrapping around the tree and killing both him and Jenna, the car hit the ground barely inches from the tree. I heard Michael pop the clutch and jam first gear as the T-Bird, spewing gravel and dirt twenty feet into the air, shot back out onto the road. He slammed on the brakes and looked at Jase and me with steeled eyes.

"Sixty-five. I win," he said without the slightest hint of emotion.

Jenna was sitting in her seat grabbing the dash, her face white as snow.

"God *damn* it, Michael," I screamed, "you're crazy!"

Jenna, pale and shaking, shot me a look that tore out my heart.

"Leave him alone! Can't you see he's in pain?" She placed her hand on his and kissed him on the cheek. "Come on, Michael, let's go."

Without a word, he floored the accelerator and roared off.

"Go ahead," I yelled at the fading taillights. "Get yourselves killed for all I care!"

Tippy came over and put her arm around me as Jase said, "Tough break, man."

I didn't know if I was angry with Michael because he stole my girlfriend or because he was acting like he had a death wish. *Hell*, I thought to myself, *girls were easy to replace*. Besides, I was never sure if I really loved Jenna or not. After all these years, I understand how difficult it is for the average person to truly recognize *love* when it is freely given to them—oftentimes, they take for granted its sheltering ambiance until it is removed and they are rendered bereft of its protection and comfort. The comprehension of love's presence, only in those moments when it has absconded forever, are perhaps the darkest moments in human history.

After driving around for a couple of hours, I decided to cruise over to Jenna's house just to see if she'd had Michael take her home or had gone out to Sugar Creek.

I drove up Parcae Avenue with my lights off afraid that they might shine on Michael's car and send me into a jealous rage. As I neared Jenna's house, I saw her bedroom light on. Parking the car on the side of the road, I snuck up to her window and tapped gently. Almost instantly the curtains parted, and she opened the window.

"Hey, you," she said, trying to smile. For that moment, dark silence was interrupted with soft music drifting from the sill where Jenna's hand rested. I didn't recognize the melody, though it seemed smooth and familiar.

"Hey Jen. Sorry I got so hot-headed earlier, but Michael scared the hell out of me." I swallowed hard trying not to sound nervous. "I was afraid he might get you both killed."

"Yeah." When she spoke, I could tell she'd been crying. "He scared me too. That's why I had him drop me off."

"You okay?" I reached out and stoked her hair gently. She closed her eyes and rested her head in my palm.

"I don't know. Right now, I'm just a little confused."

"Why?" We stood, me outside in the dark, and she in the soft light of her room, holding hands.

"I thought we were just," she dropped her eyes, and sniffed fighting back more tears, "friends. I'm not sure if I'm ready for anything, you know, serious."

Ice water shot through my veins as I realized the truth. I had been dating her exclusively, but she had not been faithful in return. The weekends we had not gone out, I now knew, she'd been with someone else. I didn't know what to say. On the one hand, if I pried, I'd come off as a jealous jerk, but if I didn't assert myself in some way, let her know I wanted something more, I'd come off as a weak fool. Somehow, saying the words I thought she might want to hear scared me more than Michael's craziness.

"Jen, we are friends." I settled for a compromise. "I love you but can't force you to feel the same." She raised her eyes and smiled. "I will, however, be here when you are ready. And if that day doesn't come, well, we'll still be friends. Nothing can change that." She gave me one of the wettest, most passionate kisses I think I've had. We stood, our foreheads together, looking into each other's eyes. At that moment, I did love her.

"I've never done it with anyone but you." She tilted her head back and rolled her eyes comically and laughed, "Well, and that one time with Michael, but," she kissed me again, "I was thinking about you the whole time."

"So," I said, returning her kiss, "see you tomorrow?"

"Yeah." She squeezed my hand and we kissed once more. Suddenly, I recognized the music from Jenna's bedroom: it was "I Just Wasn't Made for These Times" by The Beach Boys. Those melodic words both touched and stung me.

"We'll go out to Sugar Creek," I managed to say.

"Yes," said Jenna. For a while she seemed to think.

I realized, though we both were thoughtful persons with so much life before us, that something old and sad had somehow settled within each of us. It was irretrievable. Jenna looked at me in a way that said she understood how I felt. No one else could.

Instead, she said nothing, except a single utterance. "Just the two of us," she spoke softly.

CHAPTER ELEVEN

April 1970

IN 1965, some enterprising individuals in Noble built a skating rink about half a mile outside the town proper on the northern leg of Highway 37, but still within the town boundaries that seemed to inch outward a little further every year. Michael, Jase and I, along with our gal pals, spent a lot of our free time there.

One of the reasons we spent so much time skating was because the exercise helped us keep in shape. We also went there to pick-up dates, not that we had a hard time finding someone to fool around with at Sugar Creek or the Noble Horse Barns. This was especially true of Michael: countless peony-mouthed girls, all of them born and bred in this small farming community, seemed drawn to him after Caryn died. Maybe it was this visible aftertouch of tragedy—an insouciant photosphere that, for those of us who knew best, merely conveyed the deeper and more unsettled flame within him—that made Michael so enticing to Noble teenaged girls. Anyway, Michael just used them for his own pleasure before passing them on to the next guy.

After Caryn died on Halloween 1969, Michael went into a shell and seemed to be hellbent on self-destruction. The night after he took Jenna on that maddening joy ride down Carrion Road, his little T-Bird nearly got creamed by two eighteen-wheelers while drag racing Billy Western on Highway 37 with his headlights off. How he ever got that car to fly between those trucks without a scratch has baffled everyone ever since. Billy wasn't so lucky.

His car got off on the shoulder where he lost control and flipped end over end down the slope. The way I heard the story, Michael didn't even stop to check on Billy, but just floored the accelerator and kept driving. Possible, I guess. Michael didn't like Billy much because he'd tried to rape Caryn when she was fourteen. Even though Michael whopped the tar out of Billy that night, he held a grudge, and once Michael had a grudge to settle, he never let go. Michael's enemies seemed to "find justice" in odd ways.

Some of our classmates speculated that the entire incident out on the highway had been arranged. There were whispers that Michael was the leader of some "shadow group," and he hung around with Jase and me as cover. We'd all read stories about Al Capone and other gangsters and knew that such leaders always needed alibis. I didn't believe these local legends, of course, though the idea did pop into my mind occasionally, especially when Michael would disappear, sometimes for days, without a word. One reason for the rumors was because of what happened shortly after he met Caryn back in '68.

This is how it went down the first time.

Caryn and Michael had been together about a month or so. We were all sitting at our usual table near the rear of Esposito's Pizza having dinner and fooling around. Michael had gone up to order a fresh pitcher of root beer when Billy Western and his group of Cools came in.

"Jase, go help him get the root beer," Tippy said, pushing him out of our booth.

"Okay, already. I'm goin, I'm goin."

Jase had barely stood up when Billy yelled, "Well, if it isn't Booboo Bear. There's no one to help you out of this like last time."

I raised an eyebrow. The last time Billy and Michael had tangled they were the only ones present aside from Caryn. To me, the statement made no sense. I reckoned that Billy had told a different story to his gang-of-fools in order to maintain his reputation as chief reprobate.

"Back off, Silly Willy!" Jase was moving slowly towards Michael, his switchblade already out.

I sighed, looked at Jenna, who grimaced and said, "Oh, well." I knew what that tone meant, so I stood up and took out my own switchblade ready for a rumble. Usually, I was the one pulling Jase off some jerk who'd gone and looked at him cross-eyed or something, but on rare occasions, I covered his back. By that time, we both had our share of scars. Everyone else in the parlor moved out of their seats and stood as close up against the walls out of harm's way. They knew when Jase and I were in a fight that it was best to give us room.

Michael didn't move. (Come to think of it, until that night, I'd never actually seen Michael fight, *ever*.) With his back to Billy and his thugs he just stood at the counter talking casually to Janet, another classmate of ours who had worked the counter at Esposito's ever since she was twelve. As I came up beside Jase, sweat was pouring out of me like a faucet turned to full volume. I was nervous but felt good knowing that if I was going to die at least I'd die with my friends.

Then the strangest thing happened; Caryn came up to me and said, "It's okay. He can do this alone." And she insisted that Jase and I sit back down, which we did. I can't explain it, but when Caryn asked us to do something, we just did it, without question. Like Michael said many times, *the girl has something magical about her*. Well, naturally, when Billy saw us taking our seats he started laughing.

"Looks like your butt-buddies are too chicken to help you, Booboo!"

Michael still didn't do anything. I could tell Janet was scared because she backed away from her side of the counter, her eyes tremulous and wide. Bud, one of the owners of Esposito's, came out of the back carrying a baseball bat.

"You punks best be getting out of here!"

Bud, at six foot six weighing I don't know what, was bigger than Billy, but older and slower. Bud was cool and in pretty good shape for a man pushing seventy-three. One day Jenna and I were having pizza, and no one else was in the parlor, so Bud joined us. "Pizza okay?" he asked kindly.

"Best in the state, Bud."

He chuckled, looked at me and Jenna, and smiled.

"You make a pretty good couple," said Bud kindly if (I thought) a little inadvertently. "Reminds me of Jeannette and me sometimes." I wasn't sure if he was really thinking about us or not.

Jeanette was the real owner of Esposito's, and I reckoned that in her youth she was a looker. She and Bud had been living together ever since she'd lost her husband back in '65. Looking back with an older eye that can better see through the routines and cantankerousness that often envelop older relationships, I can understand: despite the surface fussiness that I noticed between Bud and Jenny, they were the happiest (and, privately, perhaps the most carnal) couple in Noble, Indiana.

"Shut up old man!" bellowed Billy. "This is between Bear and us!"

Michael nodded to Bud, who raised an eyebrow and lowered his club.

Everything seemed to happen in slow motion. Billy reached out to grab Michael by the shirt, and the next instant was flying backwards out the front door. Michael was standing on one foot, the other sticking out horizontally, spinning slowly around. He lowered his leg, faced Billy's friends, and grinned.

Tippy started laughing madly and pointed at one of the thugs who I noticed had gone and wet himself like a baby. Michael stood, his feet planted firmly, and grinned evilly at Billy's thugs. His eyes seemed to darken. For a brief moment, he was the specter of death himself.

The thugs, obviously stunned, backed slowly out the broken doors, collected Billy from off the pavement where he lay unconscious, got in their cars and drove off. Michael grabbed the pitcher of root beer off the counter, walked over to our booth, sat down and said happily as if nothing had happened, "Who's thirsty?"

After that day, Michael was called "Godfather" by our classmates, and they paid him the utmost respect. Michael and Billy tangled a few more times after that. I suppose Billy just wasn't smart enough to know when to leave something alone, with Michael coming off without a scratch every time.

"One of these days," Michael said after each fight, "Billy's going to get his, *permanently*."

I still find it hard to believe that Michael could have planned to have Billy murdered. It's more the stuff of small-town lore than actual fact. Also, not everyone in town liked Michael, and some might have traduced his character through the spreading of lies and half-truths about him. Most likely, the entire incident was a fluke, and Michael's irresponsibility finally caused someone to get killed.

No charges were ever filed against Michael, and most people soon forgot the incident.

As I said, a lot of girls were flocking to Michael's door after Caryn got hit by that train. Every time we went to the skating rink, Michael would leave with a different girl. By 1970, a lot of guys had momentary girlfriends usually picked up at the skating rink or down to the Themis

Theater—except for Jase, who'd been dating Tippy exclusively since 1968.

Jenna and I were dating other people off and on, seeing each other about once a month to catch up on gossip and such. After her night with Michael, things just seemed to get weird between us. It wasn't that we didn't love each other; more like, we were just trying different options. Anytime I'd get moody about the relationship, Michael would say, "Not to worry. You and Jenna will be married and raising your Hoosier kids in this backwater town within six months."

I had my doubts. Jenna kept talking about how she wanted to go to New York and become an actress, and I could picture her walking Manhattan streets bedizened in stardom. For myself, I was making my own plans to expunge myself from Noble forever: there was no way I'd let the town trap me like it had so many others (like Jase and Tippy, neither of whom had any plans whatsoever aside from getting married in June after graduation). Michael debated going to college or just...disappearing.

"Another acceptance letter?" Michael asked, setting his lunch tray on the table and plopping onto the bench.

"Yeah, Stanford."

"Hmmm, I got one of those."

Michael was the luckiest of our group. He got girls without trying, pushed the limits of safety tempting death to try and take him, and received college acceptance letters without even applying.

"I sent them a letter saying I'd think about it," he said casually.

Michael was a certified genius. He never, in our entire school career, received any grade for anything lower than an 'A'. In seventh grade, he had built a working computer from spare parts he bought at Noble Hardware that also carried electronic equipment for people in town who had Ham Radios in their homes. He received his first college acceptance letter about a month after winning the science fair. However, his parents insisted that he graduate from high school first. Maybe, if they had allowed him to enter college early, he never would have met Caryn, and all that followed would never have happened.

"I really wish people would just leave me alone," he'd say each time an acceptance letter arrived. "I have other plans for my life."

"Like trying to get yourself killed?" I joked.

"Screw it," he said, pushing away the tray with his half-eaten lunch, "There's nothing here for me. Now."

I thought he meant the town, but what he really meant was living.

"Why not go to college?" I urged, trying to get him focused on his life rather than thinking about death. "Hell, you can go anywhere you wish."

"Because," explained Michael as patiently as he was able, "I don't feel like being bored to tears by some pontificating jerks that have nothing to teach me anyway."

That much was true. Michael already knew more than the professors at Noble State College who were always trying to get him to come give lectures about philosophy and other topics. Still, I knew Michael's attitude was untenable and dangerous. I tried to convince him otherwise.

"A degree can open doors. The world is changing. In order to survive, you are going to need some kind of formal training." I finished the sentence even though I knew that he wasn't listening the second I said the "S" word. Formal training, hell! He was already more widely published in professional journals than most of the tenured professors in the state. His parents kept him in public school so he could have a normal childhood learning social skills instead of possibly becoming some puppet of a government think tank, or worse, which had been working out just fine until Caryn died. Erudite though he was, all of these things had compounded Michael's already quixotic nature: he was becoming more bereft of reason and soundness of mind.

"Who says I *want* to survive," he said softly, before rushing out of the cafeteria. I didn't know what to do.

I gathered up my books and headed to the school library where I worked for the two periods following lunch. Jase and Tippy strolled in holding hands and laughing as usual. God, sometimes the way they behaved was insufferable. When Jase saw my face, he grimaced.

"Been talking to Mikey again, I see."

Jase was never book smart, like Michael and me, but he knew more about people and interacting with them than most. Everyone seemed to take to him right away. He could talk for hours with the pseudo-cowboys at the Noble Barns about 'practical matters,' as he called them. He also knew that the only way he'd get anywhere in life was with his hands or back-breaking manual labor. Sometimes, I felt guilty about talking to him about my plans for college. I could almost see them living in the Noble Slums, working for minimum wages, raising yet another generation of redneck children. It boggled my mind how they could be so damn happy.

"Um, yeah, we were...."

"Yeah, I know, you were tryin' to convince him to go to college again," said Jase. "Give it up, man. Michael's a lost cause. Until he gets over Caryn, he'll just be a basket case."

So true. Caryn had become Michael's reason-for-being. Without her, he was...different.

Darker, like a shadow.

But he was still, my friend.

"Damn it, Jase," I snapped a little more agitated than intended. "How long is he going to mourn? He's been with I don't know how many girls since November! And still...he needs to snap out of it already. I am not going to give up."

"Hold on," Jase yelled, looking a little insulted and taken aback. "I didn't mean it like that."

"Hey guys," Tippy said, stepping between us as she sometimes did. "Ease up. We just need to get Michael into something fun for a change. Look, there's a big party at the rink tonight. Jase can bring some shine, and Jenna and I will bring some girls. We'll get wasted. Just like old times. How about it?"

Tippy was right, it had been a long time since we'd all been together for some actual fun. Most of the time we'd go to the skating rink, split up, meet some dates, and leave, pairing off to our own little worlds. And we hadn't really spent much time together since December, outside of chatting at school and the barns on rare occasions.

"Sounds fine," I said. "Jase and I will pick up Michael and we'll meet you and Jenna at the rink around seven."

"Perfect." Tippy kissed Jase. "I'm going to go find Jenna and see who else we can round up to put a smile back on Michael's face."

As she bounded out of the library, Jase whistled in admiration of her navy-hosed legs that careened beneath an ocherous-colored miniskirt whose pleats seemed to swish and bounce. Jase seemed lost in a dream: I thought he had forgotten me when he spoke, "Damn man, you know, if I ever lost her, I'd die."

He smiled, but I saw a shadow cross his face momentarily.

I blinked.

Someone walked by in the hallway with a radio blaring Jim Morrison's, "The End," and a chill raced through me. I thought I heard Caitlyn's voice whispering, "...*danger outside of town...*."

Then Jase slapped me on the back and said, "When you and Jenna gonna stop actin' stupid and decide to go ahead and get married?"

"Probably never."

I felt a great weight come over me. Even though Jenna and I were still seeing each other now and then, we were steadily growing apart. I knew it and she knew it. However, Jase and Tippy seemed to be blind to the situation. They were so utterly in love that they figured everyone else should be in love. I did still love Jenna; I just wasn't sure I liked her well enough to keep around forever. Some of the girls I'd bedded since our semi-split were prettier and better in bed than she could ever hope to be, and one in particular I was beginning to think a little more seriously about. But since she was going to be out of town that weekend, I figured one more roll with Jenna would be okay.

***

Most roller rinks were transformed by the Disco craze when mirror balls, bombastic lights, and modern music began to appear. The Noble skating rink wasn't a disco roller then, so the ambiance was staider and music (when there was some) hardly danceable. Plus, roller skates then were nosier, so everything was sometimes louder even when the music wasn't.

However, what the Noble rink lacked in atmosphere, the opportunities for companionship were first rate. At the corners of the wooden platform, there were always older children and teenagers in rented skates talking with others from our school. And there were plenty of dolled girls—you only had to bump them (preferably without tumbling them over) to start a conversation. If only we could find someone who looked like Caryn, we might be able to get back the Michael we'd grown up with.

"All right, guys, what's going on?" Michael said, as we leaned on the brass railing watching a crowd of teenagers, and preteens, skating around. We'd been there an hour and not one girl had even looked at Michael. Something about that was strange.

"Relax, Mikey. Tippy and Jenna are bringing along some friends, and after we skate a little bit, we're heading out to Sugar Creek for a pre-graduation party."

About that time, Tippy and Jenna entered with three other girls. Jenna was dressed in a short black dress, and black calf boots. She had her hair braided into a ponytail and had colored it a light brown. I found myself getting excited about being alone with her later. In a small way, she reminded me of Caryn the first time I met her.

Déjà vu.

Tippy, as usual, wore a different box-pleated skirt and sleveless blouse. Her short black hair and the bangs cut even with her eyebrows hung loose. She bounced up to Jase and gave him a wet kiss. They had brought Janet, the blonde waitress from Esposito's; Becky, a redheaded freshman who had a reputation for dating older guys; and Julie, a strikingly pretty brunette, who was on the high school cheerleading squad.

Michael hadn't, to my knowledge, dated any of them, and as I looked them over in their (at least for Noble) prurient outfits, I figured if all three of them couldn't snap Michael out of his death wish, then he was truly a lost cause.

I leaned back on the bar, trying my best to look casual, expecting Jenna to walk on over and claim me, but instead she seemed to float up to Michael, her eyes—lined in black had a distinctive oriental appearance—locked onto his. As she approached, she licked her lips that were covered in glossy black lipstick, hugged him and placed a long, wet kiss on his lips. From the way he reacted, I think he thought she *was* Caryn.

Everyone in the group looked on in shock, especially Tippy and Jase, who looked at me with confusion all over their faces. Janet, Becky, and Julie gave each other confused looks, shrugged and headed into the dressing room to put on their skates.

I just spun around and hit the floor, racing as fast as I could around the rink, my hair flying in the artificial breeze, and fumed. Every time I passed by Jenna and Michael they were kissing. Leaning into the curves, I increased my speed. Everyone was on the floor now skating and chatting, except Michael and Jenna who just stood against the railing, locked in that damn embrace. Veering around a curve, I slipped, but Tippy and Jase caught me by the arms and set me upright.

"Easy there, bud. Slow down."

Tippy had her arm wrapped tightly around mine forcing me to skate slower.

"I guess you won't be coming out to Sugar Creek with us then." She had a way of stating obvious things as if they were religious revelations.

"No. Reckon not."

Becky rolled up beside us and grabbed my hand. "Come on, skate with me."

We stayed until the rink closed up at midnight. Jenna and Michael had already left. Jase, Tippy, and I, with Becky in tow, decided to go on out to Sugar Creek anyway.

"They're probably already there waiting on us, bud. I'm sure, once she sees you with Becky, she'll come back to ya."

Jase and Tippy just wouldn't ease up on the situation. No matter what happened, they kept thinking that Jenna and I would still get together, permanently. Well, secretly, I hoped so too. Seeing her getting all mushy on some other dude—my best friend for crying out loud—made me want her. I thought about Jenna and Michael grunting together, and my jealousy grew.

"Yeah, sure." I snapped. Then quite sharply, I added, "Why the hell was she dressed up like Caryn?"

Becky threw up her hands and said, "That's it, I'm outta here!"

She saw Janet and Julie getting into a car with some guys they'd met earlier and yelled, "Hey! Wait up!" I didn't care. My thoughts were filled with Michael and Jenna, kissing, grunting, and screaming in fervent pleasure. I got in the GTX and floored it, spewing gravel as it bounced onto the highway towards Noble.

I drove around for a while trying to calm down. What the hell was I angry about anyway? I was only going to use Jenna for momentary pleasure that weekend. So what if she decided to have a flirt with Michael?

"You're a fucking idiot," I said out loud. "They're my friends. Friendship is more important than who bangs who."

Just as I was about to drive home something weird happened. I had been half-heartedly listening to the local AM rock station when a strangely, hypnotically sweet familiar, female voice came over the speakers.

"I'm Cloe on WFTE, your late-night queen of fate, here with you until dawn. Our next song, from the Broadway Rock Opera by the same name, is a special request going out from Cassandra to the triumvirate, "Jesus Christ Superstar." *Heed the need.*"

I braked, sliding to a stop at the corner of Sherman Road. The interior of the GTX suddenly filled with the scent of roses and violets, Caryn's scent. Caryn's mother's name was Cassandra, like the woman in Troy doomed to see the future but not have her predictions believed. My hair felt like it was standing on end as the song blared.

Vujaday!

"Every time I look at *you*, I don't understand. Why *you* let the things *you* did get so out of hand…."

Caitlyn's voice screamed in my ears, *"Danger! Hurry!"*

I covered my ears blocking out all sounds trying to concentrate. A shadowy form appeared in the seat beside me. Caryn's ghostly hand stroked my face as she whispered, "The bond is breaking. Hurry before it's too late…."

Then she was gone. The song on the radio continued as if on a loop.

"Damn it!"

I floored the accelerator and headed towards Sugar Creek. A weird fog fell as I raced the five miles down Sherman Road to the Sugar Creek Cemetery, my speedometer pegging 100, and there was, absolutely, no other traffic on the road. Something, I don't know what, kept tugging at my thoughts.

"Shit!" I yelled, suddenly realizing, "Billy's thugs, oh shit, shit, shit!"

There had been some talk at the rink that Billy Western's group of losers were planning a long-awaited revenge against Michael, but I'd been so preoccupied I hadn't really been listening. None of us had been listening…to anything.

When I arrived at the Episcopal church parking lot, my headlights fell on five cars, two of which I recognized as Michael's and Jase's. Even before I got completely out of my car, I heard female voices screaming. The song kept playing, louder than I thought it had been turned up. "…Jesus Christ! What have *you* sacrificed?!"

Then, Jase's voice screaming, "TIPPY!"

"Awwww, hell!" I yelled, as I ran towards the screams.

They were in the dark by one of the crypts. I could barely see, but what I did see terrified me. Jenna was up against a tree screaming, Jase was on his knees, holding something and rocking back and forth, Michael was surrounded by six shadows, each one carrying clubs and swinging at him.

The air suddenly split wide open with the screams of sirens. Of all the shadows, the one most malevolent in shaped shouted, "This ain't over, Bear! Next time you're dead! Split dudes."

The shadows ran towards the parking lot, and I ran to intercept Michael who was giving chase. Rearing back my fist and swinging with all the pent-up anger I'd been holding in, I punched Michael in the gut sending him tumbling to the ground. Lying on his back, he looked up at me, blinked and mouthed in a surprised manner, "Damn." It was the only time since we met, so long ago, that I'd raised my fist in anger towards him.

"STAY PUT!"

He was coughing, and I knew I'd knocked the air of him.

I ran over to Jenna, grabbed her shoulders, and slapped her face hard until her involuntary screams abated. Hugging me tightly, she breathed against my ear, "You're late."

I kissed her forehead and brushed some tangled hair out of her face. "Sorry."

Sensing my hurt, she tilted her head back and sighed heavily.

"Jealous fool. We never made any promises, and besides, I thought," she looked down, "I just thought that I'd try to help Michael forget about Caryn." When she looked at me, I wanted to kick myself. "I really didn't think you'd mind."

"Aw hell, Jen, hush." I hugged her close. "Don't...."

"We didn't *do* anything." Sighing in exasperation she continued, "We've never done anything. Just talked. All he ever does anymore is talk. *About* Caryn. Haven't you noticed? Why do you think some of the girls aren't seeing him anymore?"

I frowned.

"You're not a girl so you can't understand. When you give yourself to someone who just keeps yelling another girl's name as you..." she pressed closer to me, starting to cry, "...you just can't imagine."

Holding her tight, I turned to look towards Jase who, I could now see, was holding Tippy close and rocking back and forth. I saw that her arms hung limp, and I cursed under my breath. He looked at me, tears flooding his face, tilted back his head, and yelled, "TIPPY!" God, the way he cried and screamed scared the living hell out of me. I'd never, not even Cassandra's screams after Caryn had been hit, heard anything so heart rending than Jase's screams bubbling through a never-ending stream of tears, diluting the blood covering his shirt.

I looked around frantically for Michael and saw that he was gone. *Damn it! He'll kill them* I thought in horror.

"Go! Go," Jenna said, pushing me away. "Don't let him do anything stupid! Hurry. Hurry, darling, please."

I spun out of the parking lot just as three police cruisers slid into a braking halt, none giving chase. I saw that one of the officers was a short woman with bushy brown hair and a too familiar face, who, I swear, winked at me.

Double déjà vu…

What the…How the hell? I thought suddenly but dismissed the questions as I started thinking about how to find Michael.

I drove around until well past dawn with no luck, so I pulled into the Kroger parking lot and phoned Jase's house from the pay phone.

"Hello, Mrs. Quinn, it's me, have you heard from Jase?"

There was a long pause and she said in a quivering voice, "He's asleep. Heavily sedated. Is Michael with you?"

"No. I couldn't find him. Did you speak with Jenna?"

"Yeeees, she…she told us what happened." She started crying, "You've *got* to find Michael."

"Where's Jenna?" I asked.

"Sitting with Jase. She refused to leave. You've *got* to find *Michael*."

There was only one place I knew left to try. When I pulled onto Parcae Avenue, I saw his T-Bird parked out front of Caryn's house. Outside I heard something that sounded like the soft chimes of Tibetan singing bowls. The front door was open, so I walked on in. Inside, a Himalayan meditation record was playing and candles were lit around the coffee table. Michael was sitting on the sofa, Caryn's mother holding him in her arms. She looked up when I came in, smiled sadly, and said, "You got my message."

I raised an eyebrow.

"Still, you were late." She closed her eyes. "If only. But that is of no matter, now. Please, sit."

Her blue eyes appraised me. I felt dirty, guilty, exposed.

"What should have been light is now in shadow, and the shadow grows. However, there is still, hope. Free Will is the only random element."

"How long has he been here?" I had to know what he'd done.

"A few minutes." She smiled, "You stopped him, but…."

I didn't know what else to do. Michael's eyes were fixed on something only he could see. So, I sat down, and waited.

"Please," Cassandra said, "have some tea. It'll help."

As I sat sipping the tea, I heard Michael say in a bare whisper, "They will pay for this, Cassy. I *swear* it."

I shuddered. "Michael, let it go. The police can handle this."

He looked at me. When I looked into his eyes, I saw nothing but a deep void. "No, they can't. But I know who can."

"Let it go, man. Think. What would Caryn want you to do?"

But I could see he wasn't listening. I didn't blame him. Part of me wanted to hunt those cowards down myself, but something held me back, as if little arms encircled me, and a sweet voice whispered softly in my ear, saying, vengeance is reserved for another.

Cassandra said, "Our choices shape our futures. Which way will you turn?"

Michael closed his eyes. Cassandra lowered her head and wept silently.

I took Michael home and stayed with him until noon. He never spoke, just sat in the living room staring blankly at the fireplace, watching the flames and the dancing shadows they cast. When I went over to his house that evening after supper to check on him, his parents said he'd gone out of town for a few days.

"He's taking a tour of Stanford," his father told me. And that was the end of it.

I don't know if he had anything to do with what happened during the next three weeks, but I suspected. One by one, Billy's thugs met with some kind of "accident." Well, that's what all the official reports say anyway. Jase dropped out of school and went to live with some relatives in Kentucky.

Our little group that had been together for thirteen years unofficially disbanded. Michael's parents were killed in a freak accident shortly before graduation. Afterward, Michael vanished. The next time I heard from him was a letter from Vietnam. He said when his tour was over, he'd come visit. I didn't hold my breath.

Jenna went to New York, and after performing in a few off-Broadway shows ended up working as a waitress somewhere in Greenwich Village. I enrolled in journalism school at Indiana University in Bloomington, not far from Noble.

Sometimes, I ran into Jase whenever I went home to visit. He looked older every time and seemed grimmer. We never talked about Tippy. I could tell he was trying the best he could to forget her but knew deep down that he never would. Like Michael, he'd lost his true love.

I'd yet to find mine.

CHAPTER TWELVE

LEARNING TO FORGIVE

GROWING UP semi-poor in southern Indiana in the 1960s wasn't so bad. My friends and I spent our time collecting empty soda bottles for money, or pulling our rickety mower around the neighborhood cutting grass for five-dollars a yard. When we were older, we cleaned out stalls at the county horse barns where our parents boarded our horses, and helped the men during the summer bailing and stacking hay.

Back then twenty-dollars bought a lot more than it does today.

I only had two close friends growing up: Jase and Michael. Michael was an only child of one of the town's wealthiest families and Jase was one of six children whose father was the town drunk. My family was somewhere in the middle, not exactly poor, but not as well off as Michael's. Two things brought the three of us together: Our love for horses and adventure. We certainly were not mindful of our actions, as perhaps we should have been, but never did any of us get into any serious trouble. I once asked Michael how it was that we never landed in the middle of snakes as we swung on the vines in the woods, dropping off from ten or more feet in the air into the bushes below. His answer was somewhat cryptic: "I don't know, man. Maybe we all have some supernatural forces looking out for us." Then I saw his eyes twinkle, and not for the first time my blood froze beneath his steady gaze.

In the years following the time when the government took our classmate Lloyd away from his mother, my friends and I began spending time with one of the girls from that same class.

Jenna had been sent home from school because the nurse had found lice in her hair. Although some of the other kids in the class made fun of her and Lloyd, I thought she was pretty in a modest way. By eighth grade I started dating her, informally, and we continued our relationship on and off until graduating from high school.

After high school, my friends and I found ourselves going in different directions. Michael headed to the west coast for college someplace in Washington state, Jenna moved to New York City for a fresh start, and I went to Indiana University as an undergraduate and then enrolled as a graduate student at a land-grant college in the deep south. After a brief sojourn in Kentucky, Jase returned to Noble where he eventually became a well-known building contractor.

For nearly twenty-seven years, we saw little of each other—none of us spoke about Lloyd or Jenna. Both seemed to disappear from our knowledge.

Then came the news of Jase's death.

I spent the evening before Jase's funeral with Michael and Jenna at Michael's parent's house where we ate pizza, drank beer, and sang old songs honoring the memory of our long-time childhood friend. Early in the morning, around four or so, after the friendly neighborhood police came by to share a beer and remind us to keep the noise to a low roar, I drove Jenna to the mortuary to pick up her car. We sat in my GTX—the same one I bought from Michael after his girlfriend Caitlyn died back in 1969—and for a time we talked about our lives, and our one-time love for each other. Although she'd aged well, there was a sadness in her tired eyes that I could not reach or understand. Perhaps it was because of dreams deferred or lost, or forgotten. I don't know. In a way, I still had feelings for her I dared not expose, because we were both married.

"So, did you find her?" she asked as we stood beside her rental car, holding hands and trying to part, but neither of us wishing to go.

"Who?" I asked.

"Your one true love, of course, silly." I still loved the way she tilted her head back to laugh. How many times had I kissed her neck, still strong and firm? I almost kissed her then.

I simply told her that I was married to a wonderful person, and that yes, we were very much in love with each other.

"That's good." She lowered her eyes, not even hiding the tears. "I will miss Jase. He used to write to me when no one else did. His letters helped me through a lot of tough times. He even sent me some money one time when I was about to lose my apartment...."

All we could do was hold each other. Life had once again made its way from the end back to the beginning.

"You're always on my mind, no matter who I'm seeing," she said, giving me a kiss on the lips that I could not return. "I guess a girl never forgets her first love. But, you always did seem to be…someplace else."

Her last words cut me like an accusation. The only girl who had ever been on my mind was Caitlyn. And always will be. I think Jenna had known that all along.

"Guess I'll see you at the funeral then." She slid into her car and drove slowly away as I stood stiff-legged watching.

It was early, and I was in no mood to go back to my parent's home where I'd sleep in my old room, tossing and turning on the bed remembering, so I decided to drive over to the Steer Restaurant and have breakfast.

I walked into the restaurant and took a seat at the counter where Dad and I used to sit while he flirted with the waitresses. A pretty, if sad, Becky placed a cup of coffee before me.

"Hey you. Sorry to hear about Jase. He did a lot of good things for Noble."

"Hi Becky," I said, "How are you these days?"

"Oh, the usual, married, four kids, a husband who drinks too much…." She tried to smile, brushing back her bushy red hair going gray. "I've read your books." There were tears in her eyes as she said, "So much has changed."

I flipped through my tattered notebook. I've written a lot of stories over the years, the first one way back in sixth grade. Even so, something odd tugged at the back of my mind as if saying, "You're not finished with Noble yet."

When I went to visit Cassandra the day before, she'd told me Michael was in town. I asked her how she knew. "I felt his presence when he arrived." Then she looked at me with those deeply knowledgeable blue eyes and said, "Soon, it will be time to reveal what has been hidden in shadow too long, but not yet. I see you at your cabin near a lake, a broken bond that should not be broken. Three visitors…" then she stopped and raised an eyebrow, "one friend and two strangers, but one of them, not a stranger." I can't be sure, but I thought I saw a hint of a smile on her lips.

Cassandra was still uncanny at times.

Becky brought me a western omelet with a side of crisp hash browns. As I ate, my thoughts began churning with memories. Jase's death brought all our childhood memories rushing to the surface like a dam bursting from high explosives. In one moment, I was in kindergarten, The Themis theater, Sugar Creek Cemetery, in the GTX racing Michael in his T-Bird and Jase in his Roadrunner down backroads, galloping horses and jumping downed trees, holding Jenna as Jase screamed while holding Tippy, and watching in horror as Caitlyn....

"Jenna said you might be here."

I turned around. Behind me, with his hands in his pockets and a look of depressed happiness on his face, was someone I didn't know, but who looked familiar. In a far corner, another waitress with bushy brown hair stopped in mid-motion as she wiped a table, turned and winked at me. Before I could step off my stool and confront her, she disappeared rapidly into the back. The man touched me on the arm gently to get my attention.

"Please. I need a few moments of your time. May I join you?"

He stuck out his hand and said pleasantly, "I'm sorry. Lloyd Johnson, we attended sixth grade together."

"Lloyd?" I gazed into his eyes with sudden recognition. "Of course, yes, I remember you. Have a seat."

Lloyd, dressed in a gray Armani suit, took the stool next to me. He didn't say anything for a few minutes, then looked up, staring like he used to in class, into the mirror behind the counter.

"I love Jenna more than anyone else I've ever known. She insisted we come to Jase's funeral, even though I knew what that would mean." He closed his eyes and said tiredly, "Michael's here, isn't he?"

I raised an eyebrow. Lloyd smiled, and said, "It's okay, I'm not going to make any trouble. I love Jenna too much. I know that what happens will only be out of her love for him, and you and Jase."

Lloyd suddenly seemed like Cassandra—that is, spooky. But I let him talk without interruption. I could always tell when someone had a story, and I knew his would be important. I reached inside my jacket pocket and deftly switched on the micro-recorder I always carried. I didn't want to 'bug' Lloyd like this was Watergate or something. But I felt Lloyd was about to reveal something important for all of us. I wanted a record for later.

"Nothing is more important than true love. I'm sure you would agree." He sipped his coffee. "My parents, at least my father, never understood that. At least, I don't think he did."

As he talked, a faraway look came over his features and I could tell he was in the past.

"I was in fourth grade when they split up. It was messy. My mother, God rest her weary soul, was a saint. She walked me to school every day, brought me my lunch and sat with me as I ate, never speaking, just watching me eat my tuna sandwich and smiling. After school, we'd walk to the park near our house on Capus Street in Indianapolis and watch as I'd swing or play kickball with my friends from school. Then we'd walk home holding hands, and she'd give me two cookies and a large glass of cold milk."

"My father was a heavy drinker. He often came home drunk, and accused my mother of carrying on affairs with other men. He was forty and she was barely twenty-four. Whenever they fought, I hid under my sheets, and cried and prayed for him to stop hitting her. They lived in a small town in Kentucky, called Liberty, and got married when she was fourteen after he got her pregnant. Soon after their marriage, they moved to Indy to start fresh. However, my Dad—may he be forgiven—didn't trust her because she was young. He asserted his authority by beating her. How she stood it for so long, I'll never know.

"One night, he came home and started yelling at her like always, and slapping her face, calling her a slut. Well, somehow, I found my courage and grabbed my baseball bat. I hit him hard in the leg, but he spun around, took the bat away from me and broke my arm. As I lay on the flooring crying and bleeding, my mother hit him over the head with a lamp.

"There was a lot of screaming going on, and I was sure the neighbors must have heard. How he stayed on his feet, I don't know. He wrestled my mother to the floor and began beating her. The front door was open. My mother fought her way free and ran outside screaming. I guess the police officer who arrived with his partner must have been a rookie, because when he saw my father chasing my mother with the baseball bat he shot him. They took us to the hospital and after a few days released us.

"Mom started drinking a lot. After the divorce, money was getting tight. My father was in jail and couldn't pay child support or alimony. By the end of fifth grade, we lost our house and we moved here. She took a job working the swing shift here and would sometimes bring strange men home with her. I'd pretend to be asleep, and after they went into the bedroom, I'd go outside and sit on the stoop or walk around downtown. I figured she was getting lonely. She was always talking about how we didn't have any money, cursing my father for everything, even her drinking. Sometimes, I'd pour her liquor down the sink, but she'd find out and hit me. The next day, she'd apologize saying she wasn't in control of her actions and she'd never hit me again. I wanted to run away, but I loved my mother too much and she'd already been through so much pain. So I stayed.

"One night, Sheriff Brown found me and warned my mother that if things didn't change that I'd be taken away from her. The rest you know. I found my mother a year ago. She was in prison again and sick from breast cancer. She was so thin and frail, so I didn't recognize her. She died in my arms in the prison infirmary."

I didn't know what to say. However, I did wonder what all the talk about his parents, enlightening as it was, had to do with myself, Michael or Jenna.

"So, you see," he continued, "that's why I understand Jenna so well. In some ways, she is like my mother used to be." He sipped his coffee, staring into the mirror. "I love her. She's my one true love. Jealousy destroyed my parents and our family. I refuse to let it ruin mine. That's why I'm leaving after the funeral, and Jen is staying on a few days. She needs to get something out of her system. After that, I'll have my wife back, and our lives will be better."

I was stunned. Any other man would be furious, but Lloyd, knowing his wife might be unfaithful, still had faith in her. Seeing my confusion, he laughed. Lloyd tossed five dollars on the counter and smiled at me.

"Jen is really a remarkable woman, but until she lets go of the past, she'll never be truly free." Without waiting for my reply, Lloyd walked away.

I paid Becky for my meal, leaving a five-dollar tip, and took a long drive. Everything in town looked smaller. After visiting the Sugar Creek Cemetery and placing flowers on Caryn's and Tippy's graves, I cruised over to the Noble Slums and parked on the side of the street. The duplexes had been refurbished, but basically looked the same. I walked around Crescent and Francis streets, stopping in front of our old houses, and a sign that read, Jason Hoag Building & Remodeling, remembering.

In the summer, the Mister Frosty Ice Cream truck, a big blue and white van with a curly vanilla cream cone on top, would cruise the neighborhoods. Michael, Jase, and I—along with the other kids in the neighborhood—would buy ice cream sandwiches, or popsicles that dripped cherry and banana flavors onto our hands making them sticky. We would sit on the curb, eating ice cream, joking, and feeling like we'd never grow old.

As I stood on the corner of our streets, my hands in my pockets and the wind blowing my hair, I heard the voice of a child yelling, "Dang it, Michael, Jase, wait up will ya!" Spinning around, I thought someone, or something, punched me in the arm, and I heard a voice in a sharp Kentucky accent say, "Yo, man, wake up!"

Turning again, I heard the roar of dual exhaust and saw two cars—one a metallic green GTX and the other a black Roadrunner—careen around the corner and disappear in the distance.

"Hey mister," a tiny voice across the street yelled, "you lost?"

Yes, I thought, smiling and waving to a kid in worn out blue jeans, dirty sneakers and a mangy blue muscle shirt, his long unkempt brown hair blowing, and smiling with partially rotten teeth. The kid waved back. Then turned and walked towards the backyard of one of the duplexes.

I walked back down the street, got into the GTX, and drove away.

NOTE

First published in Freedom's Hill Primer *on November 10, 2017. (Courtesy of the Carolina Institute of Faith and Culture)*

FOURTH PHASE

HOLES IN SKY

CHAPTER THIRTEEN

Two Souls, One Heart

September 1990-June 1997

NEARLY twenty years after leaving Noble and the poor inhabitants caught in its insidious web of mediocre existence, I took a new job at a small college in Nashville teaching an assortment of English classes, as well as Humanities, History, and Journalism courses to keep me actually interested in the mundane, routine world of academia. My life up to that point was unremarkable. I roamed from one college to another without an interest in tenure, and seemingly without any real direction. Most of my spare time was spent in doing either research or writing. My books—fiction, nonfiction, and a couple collections of American folklore—sold well enough to offset my modest professor's salary to the point that I mainly worked when I felt like it, taking extended sabbaticals to travel or write yet another book of empty rhetoric. Although I met a lot of interesting, if not sometimes tedious, members of the American intelligentsia and nouveau riche, as well as many even more interesting working-class people scattered throughout the small towns of America, the one thing for which I searched eluded me.

I just could not find that one special person whose soul understood mine, and mine hers, my one true love, Caitlyn.

The relationships I had since leaving Noble were empty encounters with sad women looking for perfection in men or stylized Hollywood love. Not once, in all my years of dating, did I ever find any woman for which I felt a real connection. I needed something more than physical gratification. Something magical, as Michael would have said if he'd been around.

Naturally, it did not help that I would immediately superimpose Caitlyn's face over the faces of women at the most inopportune times, such as during the climax of an especially satisfying round of intimacy while yelling Caitlyn's name loud enough to rattle the walls. Although I trained myself to keep silent during those times, I never could shake the habit of seeing her face everywhere. I felt as though I was chasing after a phantom who took pleasure in taunting me. Sometimes, in the darker hours of long lonely nights, I would toy with the idea of going to New York to find Jenna—one of my longest lasting relationships during high school—but never followed up on the idea.

As the decades drew on, I gave up hope of ever finding Caitlyn and settled for that professorship in Nashville that promised tenure within five years. Even the woman who interviewed me knew what I needed more than I did.

"The time comes in our careers when we should put aside dreams and focus on the concrete; the here and now."

I would not have taken her seriously if she had not looked so young and have such a bushy head of light brown hair. She possessed an inner spirit that seemed to radiate peace from her to me. I imagined Caitlyn chastising me for my laissez-faire attitude towards my career. Throughout the interview, my new supervisor was constantly smiling, and winking to emphasize specific points and perks of the job. The person who was always rearing his foot back to kick me in the butt whenever I made a mistake was bopping me upside of the head and saying, "Take the bloody job and go for tenure. It could be your last chance." So, I took the job and began doing what was needed in order to ensure I received tenure when the time came.

Five years later I was firmly entrenched at the college and settled in to await retirement—in about thirty years or so—and eventually, death. My life was anything if not one of (to quote Thoreau) 'quiet desperation.' During those years I did not date at all. There were women who visited my house for different reasons and provided momentary distractions I needed to keep me from losing my mind, but nobody serious enough to actually call a relationship.

For some reason, women were drawn to me at social occasions. Sometimes they were fans of my books, or just interested and eager to find out firsthand if the rumors—and I am sure there were plenty—

about my bedroom manners were true. Of course, some were just bored or neglected housewives who wanted short meaningless flings that I provided with pleasure.

It was right about that time, when I had completely given up on finding love of any kind and of ever finding Caitlyn, when Sabrina entered my life.

It was the second day of classes at the beginning of the fall semester '94. I was standing at the podium looking up at the two hundred odd students in the lecture hall with ambivalence. About halfway through my lecture about the mythology of ancient Greece, specifically, stories about the Moirai, a young blonde woman entered the hall and caused a commotion.

She came stumbling through the double doors of the lecture hall. She hadn't gotten past the John Glenn and Albert Einstein double stained glass panels before promptly spilling her armload of books, papers, and other paraphernalia across the pit before the first row of raised seats.

"Oh, poo, I'm so sorry. Let me get these."

Bending and half stumbling, she collected her things to the roaring laughter of the other students. I just stood silently by the podium watching her slim figure with fascination. From a half-kneeling position, she looked up at me, drew short brown fingers through her long curls and sighed.

"Sorry, professor, sorry. I'm so nervous."

"Quite all right, miss…"

"Sabrina. Just Sabrina."

"Take a seat please, Sabrina."

"Yes sir."

When she looked up at me, her half-moon wire-rimmed glasses had slipped down to the end of her little nose; I thought I saw her blue eyes, twinkle. Seeing an uncomfortable familiarity in her face, I blinked wondering why, for a fleeting moment, I saw Caitlyn smile and wink at me. She walked up the steps to the top row, looking back at me, smiling. I felt a rush of cool race through my body and was sure I heard Jase say in his sharp Kentucky accent, "Vujaday."

I watched Sabrina's lithe form, hidden beneath a mid-length black dress and tight calf boots, as she ascended the stairs and took a seat. Something familiar was tugging at my mind. When our eyes met, I felt a tinge of recognition, and knew that she felt it as well. As soon as she sat down, she crossed her legs and gently pushed her glasses back into position with the exact same movements I had seen Caitlyn use many times back at the printing station in junior high.

Throughout the rest of the lecture, I could not take my eyes off hers. Sabrina listened to my words as if judging me, as a master patiently listens to the apprentice before chastising him or her for forgetting some basic fundamentals. The only movement that told me she either agreed or disagreed with my renditions was a tiny twitch at the corner of her mouth. As the lecture drew to a close, I found myself speaking in a manner that seemed to beseech acceptance from her.

At the end of the class the students filed rapidly out of the hall, as most young people tend to do, eager to get their noon meal and gossip about their eccentric professor and the strange young woman who'd captured his attention.

"Professor?"

I looked up from stuffing my books and note papers into my satchel to see Sabrina standing in the pit before the podium. For some reason, I was then at a loss to understand, my blood pounded double-speed through my veins and the silver ring I'd worn on my left pinky since high school became noticeably warmer, almost hot. I looked into Sabrina's eyes, almost wanting to ask the impossible question, but biting back such an obviously insane impulse. I swear she was the spitting image of Caitlyn as I imagined she'd look at twenty-five, which meant that she could not *be* Caitlyn, because my Caitlyn would be much older. I shook my head slightly to throw back the thoughts streaming through my weary brain.

"Professor? Excuse me, do you have a minute?"

My hands began shaking. When she pronounced the words, she drew out her vowels and consonants in exactly the same manner as Caitlyn. I forced myself out of my fantasy, hoping she hadn't noticed my momentary distraction.

"Umm, yes, of course."

"I apologize for coming in late. I'm a research assistant for Doctor Marin, and I, well, lost track of time."

"So, you're a graduate student then?"

"Yes. I'm a transfer student, and when I heard you were giving a seminar on world mythologies, well, I…."

"Just had to sign up." I'd heard that line before, usually from some pre-PhD graduate hoping to pad her vita.

"I'm an artist, actually, but love learning everything I can about ancient cultures, especially their folklore. I believe art and writing—stories and pictures—tell us so much about human nature. Like love."

Typical popular rhetoric. I thought as we walked together through the double doors, down the hall, and out onto the rotunda.

"Let me guess. You've read my books and think that attending my class will...."

"Actually, I've never read your work." She interrupted, her face turning a very attractive pink. Somehow, I found the fact that she was unfamiliar with my books enticing. But not in the usual sexual manner as it had been with other women who could be seduced with midnight readings. No, there was something else about Sabrina that drew me to her.

"I believe," she continued as if speaking to a life-long friend, "that fate sometimes conspires to bring two people together. Even death cannot prevent *love eternal* from being realized."

And there it was. The last time, in fact the only time, I'd heard those exact words occurred in junior high as Caitlyn and I were printing up some flyers for a party that Michael was giving at his house. I looked into Sabrina's eyes and knew. Just knew. There was no way on earth that Sabrina could be Caitlyn, but whatever it was within Caitlyn that drew me to her now drew me to Sabrina.

"You do believe in love eternal, don't you?" She said, her eyes ebullient with hope.

The semester sped by like a whirlwind. Sabrina and I debated daily in the lecture hall, and in time our debates continued during lunch, and eventually late dinners at either her home or mine. At no time, however, did our relationship reach beyond that of colleagues—master scholar and apprentice—until the spring of '95.

It was midnight during the spring equinox. We had been listening to Miles Davis and drinking Merlot on the living room floor while warming to the heat put off by a small log quietly burning in the fireplace. Then from out of nowhere, Sabrina asked, "Do you believe in reincarnation?"

In my youth, growing up in Noble, my friends and I had experienced a lot of very strange phenomena, but I had never once even thought about the possibility of souls being reborn through cycles of spiritual evolution. As I sat with my back resting against the sofa, slowly twisting my wine glass between thumb and forefinger, mesmerized by the reflected light of the fire in the crystal, I thought about Caitlyn and the endless possibilities of existence.

Sabrina and Caitlyn had a lot of characteristics in common; however, for Sabrina to be Caitlyn reborn would mean that Caitlyn had been a ghost when I knew her in junior high. That was a possibility I did not entertain. I didn't believe in ghosts, but Sabrina reminded me a little too much of Caitlyn. I suppose that will always be the curse of a wounded heart: to superimpose the spirit of a love lost onto the soul of a love found.

"No. I guess I don't." I replied almost in a whisper. When I turned to look in Sabrina's eyes, I knew that I did love her.

Her reply was simple, if not a little mysterious to me at the time.

"Maybe you should."

We never spoke about the subject of reincarnation again.

We married on July 2, 1995. Michael returned from wherever he was then living to stand up with Jase as dual Best Men. Sabrina's father gave us a cabin on Kentucky Lake in Tennessee as a wedding present, and we settled down easily into married life with me teaching and writing, and Sabrina working on advanced degrees in art and philosophy.

After Jase died in October 1995 and Michael vanished, I began to slide into an early middle-age-crazy mood. Sabrina and I had taken to attending semi-organized philosophy meetings at Foucault's Tavern in downtown Nashville. As she and her friends carried on intense and complicated conversations about existence, I slowly sank into a world of my own until all I heard were the voices in my head while watching those neo-philosophers' silent mutterings emanating from bobbing heads. By June of 1997, I'd had my fill of Sabrina's friends and their circular psychobabble, so I packed my bags and headed to our cabin on Kentucky Lake. I left Sabrina a note saying I planned to conduct some research for a new book and do some writing, and that I'd call her at the end of June to update her on my progress. In reality, I went to the cabin to forget. And perhaps devise a way to leave Sabrina, and this crazy world, forever.

I had been looking for my one true soul mate ever since Caitlyn disappeared. After several years of marriage, to the one I thought fit the bill, I began to have doubts. So, instead of staying at home trying to work out whatever the problem seemed to be, I ran and hid. Two days after arriving at the cabin Sabrina called. She said it was good that we take some time apart.

"You need time to yourself to write and I need some solitude to finish my dissertation." As Sabrina said this, I faintly heard John Coltrane's "After the Rain" on the other end, and I felt a restorative touch reaching across the line. For a moment, I thought I could return her contact. "You'll see," she continued. "By the end of summer, everything will work itself out. I love you."

After I hung up the phone, I sat on the porch and thought about Sabrina, jazz, the beauties of water and sky. And I wondered what I had done to deserve such a perfect wife who, for some shadowy reason, seemed to be getting on my nerves.

Eventually, I was hungry, so I went inside, turned on the radio, and opened some pancake mix. All these years, I still find comfort in the sounds and aromas of breakfast food.

As I mixed water and egg into batter, I noticed the dial was on an oldies station playing "Bleecker Street." I stirred and considered Simon and Garfunkel's claim that a shadow might touch a shadow's hand. Then involuntarily, my attention turned to buttery sizzle and pancake smell.

I tried to refocus and pick up the lyrics again, but the words had ceased. All had transformed into shouting commercials for local dealerships. I poured an iced tea and whisky, put the pancakes on a plate, added syrup, and returned to the porch.

The earlier connection, if it ever existed, was gone.

CHAPTER FOURTEEN

Summer 1997

MICHAEL is what you'd call a Dark Angel or Anti-Paladin, though, in truth, no one label can accurately describe him completely. To most of the people who encounter him, Michael is an enigma, which is how he likes it. However, to me he's always just been a *friend*.

We grew up in Noble during the days of *Hippie Love* and *Leave It to Beaver* TV. While our friends were into playing soldier or watching war and Kung Fu movies—in between nightly news casts of more violence from that tiny country in Southeast Asia—Michael and I were in the library reading, and trying to get the girls *a-winking*. We also spent much of our free time hanging out at the local pizza joints talking about the many things we hoped to do with our lives.

I'm not sure why we ever became friends because, to be honest, Michael and I have always been opposites. He was the athlete; I was the scholar. That's not to say Michael wasn't smart because he was. He has an eidetic memory. Everything he reads, sees, and hears, he remembers, total recall. But he wasn't one for the books. Mostly, he just chased girls. Caught most of them too. His one true vice, as far as most of us were concerned, was his unhealthy curiosity for the occult.

Many of us back then, before our friends were sent off to Southeast Asia, liked to read stories about ghosts and the like—Southern Indiana being rife with such lore—but Michael was completely *obsessed* with it all. Not just ghost stories and folklore, but everything concerning the occult. It almost seemed as if he was trying to find a doorway to the other side.

By the time we reached high school, Michael could read and speak fluently several languages. All of which came in handy because his one main quest—besides girls—was the ancient texts he was sure contained all the secrets of the universe.

At the time, I wanted to be the steady rock of our group, and so I dismissed Michael's curiosities as a bunch of rot. Now, so many years later, as I sit in my cabin by Kentucky Lake in Tennessee, writing it all down, I'm less sure of my earlier judgment. Point of fact, I'm less sure of all the Bulverism I've absorbed from forward-looking books and modern-minded professors throughout the years.

It was nearing midnight as I sat by the computer trying to write the first chapter of a new novel, but the words were not coming as easily as they used to, when my friend dropped by for a visit. I could hear my German cuckoo clock in the kitchen sound the hour. A thick gray fog had wandered off the lake and engulfed the cabin, and an unnatural chill filled the summer air. Part of me was anticipating the arrival of my friend, almost in the same manner a married woman anticipates her illicit lover's embrace; another part feared his visit, and I don't know why, for as I have already said, Michael is my friend.

He arrived just as the clock finished striking the hour. A gentle rapping at the door preceded his entrance. As I was about to answer the knock, the door flew open and Michael strode into the living room and headed straight for the kitchen where he took a beer from the fridge and downed it in one long swallow. He then began opening and banging the cabinet doors, poking his head in here and there as if looking for something. As usual he was dressed all in black and wearing silver rimmed glasses with dark blue lenses. I watched this activity for a few minutes, fascinated by how much he seemed like a child rummaging through forbidden territory.

"What *are* you doing, old man?" I finally asked.

He appeared to be frantic yet, as always, very much in control of his emotions.

All he said was, "Where's the damn root beer?" As he poked around the cabinets, he continued to mildly fuss. "And you call this crap food? Rice, soup, doughnuts...where's the damn meat and potatoes? I smell meatloaf...okay, that's a start."

He shoved his head in the fridge and sighed. "That's a lot of beer, bud. Brandy, whiskey, beer...trying to forget something? Or do you have a death wish?"

"You judging me, Michael?" I was getting pissed.

Suddenly he stopped and looked at me as if about to say yes. Popping another beer, he leaned against the counter and drank deeply. The gemstone on his pendant seemed to glow for a moment. Crushing the empty can on the countertop, he replied, "Not me."

I didn't like the way he said that.

"Not my job. I'm just here to inspire you." He looked mentally tired. And his voice sounded like a priest telling an innocent man he couldn't save him from the gallows. "Get you back on the right path if possible."

"Fine." I replied a bit confused. "How about I fix us something to eat while you put on some music and relax?"

"Yeah…music! That'd be good. Anything except The Doors. Where's Sabbath? That'll piss them…um, never mind."

I noticed a strange tremor in his voice, as if a great burden was weighing him down, but then, Michael had always been a bit intense. Not worrisome mind you, but very, I don't know really, I guess tightly focused on what he was doing would be accurate enough. However, this time he did sound and look worried about something.

I often feel nervous around Michael. It's a feeling like soldiers get in the bush; keeps them on their toes ready to spring into action. Michael has always had a way of suddenly jumping up without warning and insisting we *'go somewhere, right now, without delay'*. In our youth, these adventures were usually exciting, and yes, dangerous, but I loved them. I don't believe my friend realizes how slow age has made me. Not that forty-five is old. I'm just not up to the challenge as I was thirty years ago.

Although we've been friends since the beginning of elementary school, he's never told me much about his life after college. I doubt he ever told our other friend, Jase, very much either. In fact, for the past several years, up to and after Jase's *'accidental'* death, Michael has lived like a recluse near Memphis. To be honest, I hadn't heard a word from or concerning Michael in more than two years. We used to talk on the phone now and then, sent cards during the holidays, but rarely visited each other after he retired to civilian life.

What I do know about his life after college is this, and these are mere facts of record: He was an officer in the Navy. Worked in Intelligence or some related field. Won several medals and spent a number of years assigned to a Special Forces unit in southern California. Beyond these sketchy details, he never uttered a word.

Then one day that dog-eared letter arrived—by special messenger—stating he wished to visit me for some, secret reason of importance.

Sure, I'd heard the rumors—from other friends still holding-the-fort back in our hometown—the cloud of mystery surrounding him and his activities, but never paid them much mind. People, after all, gossip, especially given the current political climate where we are more obsessed with government cover-ups and UFO conspiracies.

My curious side hoped Michael would tell me his stories. I wondered what adventures he'd relate. *Perhaps*, I mused, *I'd become the unnamable confidant of a super-secret government operative who knew the truth about things most of us just fleetingly become curious about.*

Then my rational side took control. Michael? Master Spy? Super-secret government deep-cover agent? Assassin? Eccentric rich kid gone recluse, yes. Puppet of the government, no.

In the end, I surmised Michael must have finally gotten over Jase's death, and had decided to talk about it. That was the main reason I felt nervous about his visit. I just didn't feel much like talking about Jase. But what did he mean about getting me back on the right path?

We sat in the living room eating western omelets, sausages, fried potatoes with green peppers and onions, listening to vintage Black Sabbath and drinking black coffee. There seemed to be a dark shadow over my friend. He didn't speak a word as we ate; just chewed the food slowly while staring at the front door, which was still open giving us a view of the mist covered lake beyond the pine trees.

I desperately wished to know what it was he wanted to discuss with me, but knowing him as I did—mostly from our high school days—I figured the best thing to do was wait until he mentioned it.

Michael had a way of being far too secretive about the most ordinary things: a habit that drove off many an otherwise would-be girlfriend or potential wife. Hell, who am I kidding, I loved it. His secrets. The mysterious way he had of releasing information to Jase and me as we sat impatiently on the edge of our seats. Most of the time, after a heated build up from our friend, we'd end up being embarrassed at having our legs pulled yet again. Michael would then light a cigarette, lean back in his chair and say, "One day I'll have something real to tell, and neither of you will believe me."

"How's the wife these days?"

"Fine, I reckon." I wasn't ready for that question. It was the last thing I wanted to discuss at the time. "Is that what you wanted to talk to me about? The big secretive topic you couldn't mention in a letter."

For a moment, I was flummoxed with Michael and swore if all he wanted was to talk about my marital affairs, I'd punch him in the nose and toss his butt out the door. I reached for a bottle of Kentucky whiskey lying on the floor near my chair. As my fingertips touched the bottle, it rolled suddenly out of my reach and clinked against the far wall.

"More coffee." Michael said filling my cup. "You would be better off drinking root beer. Remember that sweet mixture we'd get at the old Dog 'n Suds?"

I drained the coffee. "Why'd you ask about my relationship with Sabrina?"

"Making small talk," he said nonchalantly.

"Small talk? That's not your style, old friend. What's really on your mind?" His face suddenly went darker. He removed his glasses, and I watched as his eyes turned from green to the darkest black. It was a look I'd never seen before (and by God I hope I never see again). When he looked at me, I could actually feel the blood curdling in my veins.

"There are few things in the universe more precious than true love," he said while looking me in the eye with a serpentine gaze that was cold and steady. "Friendship is one of them. What I have to tell you cannot be questioned. Agreed?"

I wanted very much at that moment for him to go away. Looking into his eyes, those coal black orbs that seemed to draw me into an endless void, scared me more than anything else ever had. My body froze in place as my mind screamed to run, to get far away from that place and that demon in the shape of a friend. He grabbed my left wrist in a grip that was colder than ice, yet strong as steel.

"*Truth*…is the secret I have to tell. Things that to most people are but flickering shadows on the wall. Are *you ready* to believe?"

"I'm not sure, Michael. Perhaps…maybe now isn't the right time…."

Michael put his glasses back on, mercifully covering those dead dark eyes, and leaned back on the sofa with a sigh. I felt as if I'd been far away and suddenly thrust back into my body. Bolting upright, I started for the door, tripping over the coffee table and spilling what was left of our meal on the floor. I ran down the cobbled path from my cabin to the pier. The full moon rising over the treetops looked like a skull glaring down at me. Behind me, as I crouched on the dock gasping for air, I heard heavy steps on the tired wooden planks.

I didn't move. Just waited. After all he was my friend. And what is friendship but trust?

The night was extraordinarily quiet. The only sound was that of a Zippo lighter: open, flame, close. I heard the rapid burn of the cherry and the slow exhale of smoke. Then he spoke. His voice came out in a strange monotone that seemed to carry me away on the wings of fantasy.

"I call them the Neo-triumvirate. What they call themselves, I've never known. You can be sure they have respectable titles and are upstanding citizens of the universal society where power moguls play a complicated game of chess with human lives. Their existence is known to only a few; most of them are now dead. Their ultimate purpose is unknown. They control most of the wealth and military strength throughout the world. I'm told they've been around since before Egypt fell to Alexander, operating under various names and from within secret societies, controlling one kingdom, one nation at a time. Slowly building, consolidating...preparing. But they have other interests as well. Many of which coincide with my own. They call me Darkle. And because of them...I am damned, or blessed, depending on your point of view."

I couldn't look at him. Barely believed what he was saying yet knowing for a fact everything was complete truth. The lake was still; the moon steady; the mist, although thicker, motionless. I felt as if time had literally stopped.

"Is that a polite way of saying you've committed murder?"

"Murder is an act of perverse pleasure, or misplaced, misguided sexual desire, or lack there-of. I merely removed cancers from the body of society."

"It's still killing," I tried to disparage him, but in vain. "Sanctioned by the government or not...murder is murder."

"That's only a small part of it, and not why I am damned."

"Sounds like a good enough reason to me."

"Trust me, there are things far worse."

"Okay then, why do you say you're damned?"

"Because of the things I've learned along the way. My experiences. Things that if you knew existed would turn your pretty little academic world inside out."

I relaxed a bit. This felt like more familiar territory, like the Michael I'd grown up with. I could almost feel my leg being tugged. Well, that is until I looked at his face again. The lips tight, his jaw set in a face struggling between life, death, and unyielding torment.

"Okay...thrill me."

We returned to the cabin. Michael cleaned up the dishes as I readied the recorder. We drank some coffee laced with just a taste of brandy to take off the unnatural summer chill before starting. The brandy calmed my nerves, and I found myself able to relax as Michael spoke, though his voice still sent random chills through my body.

"I'll tell you what I can about my adventures these past years. I'm sure you'll find a way to make use of them. But one story...well...for that you'll need to hear from...other sources."

"What sources?"

"During the next three weeks you'll have two more visitors. Don't worry, they know all about you. Just record what they say. When it's over I know you'll find a way to put it all together."

"Can't you tell me more? I mean...."

"No need to, you'll understand later. Now is not the time."

"All right," I said, knowing him well enough that when he started being secretive to just let him play it through. "Let's get started."

Michael stretched out on the sofa. Silence filled the room. Then he began speaking. Slow and steady, his voice carrying me off into the mists of his memories.

For six nights, Michael told me of his life. Each morning, just before sunrise, he would leave—perhaps to walk alone in the woods or return to whatever cabin he'd rented for his visit—returning an hour or so after sunset. I never asked him where he went during the day. When I told him he could stay with me, he refused without explanation. Just a simple, "No."

When we were young, Michael would often disappear for several days at a time, so I didn't make further inquiry. After hearing some of his stories, I wasn't sure I wanted to know.

CHAPTER FIFTEEN

Summer 1997

AFTER Michael left for the final time, I relaxed on the sofa for several hours. I felt violated. His tales left me drained, physically and emotionally, and my mind swirled with images best hidden. Images of demons and witches. Of vampires and cannibals. Of the most demented humans populating our dark cities whose very existence is hidden by the visible debasements of drug addicts, prostitutes, and corruption. Of secrets best left to those trained to observe and understand the supernatural aspects of life, which we who are too firmly grounded in so-called reality cannot believe exist. A numbness crept into my body, quietly sucking away at that which gives me life, like a mosquito slowly sipping blood from my forearm on a hot summer day.

I felt...*empty*. I wondered, after all I had experienced in Noble, how I had lost my faith and belief in such fringe ideas. It seemed the more research I conducted into folklore and legends, the less I believed. Too much clinical analysis and rationalizing of myths, and other impossibilities, passing them off as just stories, metaphors, and religious psychobabble had turned me into a mental zombie. Mainstream academic dogma would never accept any of Michael's tales as truth.

Since Michael's first visit, an unnatural fog filled the area during the night. I sat on the porch rocking, watching as the first rays of the sun appeared on the horizon and the fog dissipated. Three ravens began circling the lake. A frigid chill passed through my body as an ethereal female voice whispered in my ear, *"You have to believe in order to see."*

The night shades me from the day's glare. I walk barefoot to the pier where I sit, dangling my feet above the greenish, moss-covered water. Stars seem to dance above my head. I think of angels laughing. The moon, filling the eastern half of the sky just above the pine tops, illuminates me with its silvery light. I sense Danu, that ancient Celtic goddess of my ancestor's homeland, peeking from behind the trees, looking for any flaw in my spirit making me susceptible to the dark side.

Near midnight, I wander back up the brick-laden path to the cabin that smells of cigarettes and worry. Three ashtrays filled to overflowing with gray ash and yellow butts—souvenirs of Michael's visit—sit on the coffee table near the recorder and stack of tapes. As I stand in the doorway gathering my nerve, a thick fog seeps into the cabin. I stumble to the shower, letting the lukewarm water massage away all worry and concern.

After my shower, I begin to transcribe the first of the tapes. It is slow, tedious work at first; then my fingers begin to fly across the keyboard as I half-recall, half-listen to the tapes containing Michael's monotonic voice taking me behind the veil of the real.

Then she arrives.

Coffee sits cooling on my desk as I lose myself in the typing, my fingers tingling from their intercourse with the computer's keys. The German cuckoo clock in the kitchen squawks three, but I keep working like an automaton lost in the otherness of the stories rolling up the computer's screen.

The door flings open, thudding against the wall as a tall woman with gleaming white skin storms into the cabin. She paces back and forth before me, slim delicate fingers clenching, relaxing, clenching. Her waist length platinum blonde hair swirls around her face and shoulders like willows in a typhoon, the bangs cut level with her eyebrows. Her breathing comes in sharp intakes, then quick short bursts. I hear her whisper, as if speaking to someone unseen, "Who am I to judge?"

Pants of anxious desperation, uncertainty, escape her full lips painted bluish-black. Shiny white leather pumps fly from her feet as she kicks them off into the kitchen, before flinging herself down into my Rest-Easy recliner. One leg she drapes over the right arm of the chair; the other stretching out in front. They are smooth as silk with tight, flexuous muscles. She lies back in the chair with her arms spread wide and head tilting back exposing a strong firm neck.

A silver triquetra pendant hangs from a silver chain just above her breasts.

I fixate on her form. The most beautiful yet frightening woman I have ever seen. I watch as a single drop of sweat slips down her neck, disappearing between the mounds of her breasts. My eyes slowly record every inch of her semi-translucent body starting with the delicate curve of the arch of her foot slowly bouncing back and forth, up the slow curve of calf, past rounded knee, across tender welcoming thigh, over slim, flat abdomen and finally resting on full ready lips glistening in the artificial light. Her white satin dress clings to her sweating body, partially revealing what lies beneath. Her sweet aroma—violets, roses, honeysuckle and wine—approaches on cat's feet unwittingly seducing me. I sit as a statue staring at the embodiment of a Celtic goddess come to Earth.

On the ring finger of her left hand shines a silver ring with etching on the surface. The words *True Love* glow an eerie bright blue.

Michael had spoken of her beauty but had not prepared me for this vision sitting before me. Then she snaps her head forward, speaking in a melodic voice that could lure any sailor to a rocky death.

"Ma amour…ma chérie…my life…I fear it is too hard to do. Ah, Michael, is this man before me truly worthy of salvation? I wonder."

I gravitate towards her words, which I remember from years before: Roma French and all those nights back in Noble. *Caryn*? The moment the name enters my mind, the woman smiles and nods.

As she speaks, I stare into her brown oriental eyes that twinkle and sparkle like ebullient crystals in a kaleidoscope, drawing me into her very soul. My heart races, pumping blood faster through my body, until….

She laughs quietly with a small smile dancing across her lips.

"One shouldn't be ashamed of having human desires."

I feel she can read the shame on my face and smell all desires.

She lays her head back, stroking her throat with her right hand, slowly moving it up and down. Another quiet laugh escapes her lips.

"After all, men are what they are. I know…I've had *them* all."

"You *are* Robyn?" The question comes out as a hushed whisper. I'd expected an attractive woman, but not one whose beauty reached into the very heart, breadth and depth of being. There was not one single thing about her that detracted from the sexual essence emanating from her body and soul. Here, before me, was the kind of woman who could make any man or woman desire her.

"I am she. *Now* do you believe in reincarnation?"

I blink.

Our eyes lock. I begin to arouse from what had been but a momentary slumber. So soon, I thought. She smiles brightly, disarming me with her sparkling eyes and shining light that hangs about her silvery hair, suddenly becoming all business.

"Where shall we begin? I'm sure Michael told you much already."

"Wherever you wish. Actually, what he told me so far is only bits and pieces. He said you'd fill in the gaps."

An odd darkness comes over her face as her eyes narrow and she nods in understanding.

"It's voice activated," I tell her while placing a fresh tape into the recorder. "Just start talking."

As she begins to speak, head back and eyes closed, I carefully edge my way into the bathroom where I let the icy water wash away my shame. As I stand under the steady stream, I can hear her sweet, melodic voice echoing off the cabin walls.

CHAPTER SIXTEEN

Summer 1997

ROBYN told me just one story, filling in the gaps of what Michael had told or alluded to in his. I sat in my bathrobe, drinking coffee and brandy, listening intently to the story of her life. I became drunk on her beauty and her tale. I wanted more. Asked for details. Prodded her into revealing her very soul. And all the while she never moved. Except the foot bouncing gently as to a rhythm only she could hear.

For several days after Robyn left, I did nothing but sit on the porch watching the murky lake water lap up against the shore. I thought about Sabrina waiting for me in Nashville. If she were still there. Then my worries were alleviated. She called. But instead of racing to the phone like a lovesick teenager, I let the answering machine take her message. I guess a part of me doubted her sincerity.

"Hi *darling*." The background had a faint hint of Dave Brubeck playing what seemed like a Duke Ellington tribute; but what was most captivating for me was her voice: something about it naturally clears the cobwebs. Her messaged continued. "Father has asked me to come to California for the rest of the summer. I told him I would since you will be at the lake working. I hope you have been able to write up there all alone. Call me so I will know everything is all right."

Yes, I missed her. We'd been married only a few years. She is fifteen years my junior and still working on her doctorate. That had been part of the problem. The so-called friends she often had over to the house bothered me with their pedantic banter about art theory, extraneous philosophies, and twisted views of morality. We argued. Things were said. I left. Ran away to our lake house to sort things out. Trying to find a way to tell her we were through because my obsession with finding Caitlyn, if she was out there, was becoming too strong to resist. She still reminded me so much of Caitlyn, and I felt guilty staying with her for the wrong reasons. It wasn't fair to Sabrina, so I had to find a way to set her free.

But Michael and Robyn's stories had put other thoughts in my head.

Robyn's visit was short but enlightening. She got me thinking about my marriage in a new light. When I finally began transcribing her tapes, interweaving her story into Michael's, I felt a new energy and understanding fill my soul. I wrote all night, sleeping only a few hours during the day, taking time out to sit on the porch or the pier and contemplate my life.

I thought of the first time I spent the night with my wife, several months before we even began to talk about marriage when love was experienced rather than defined. We sat in her bed, drinking wine and absorbing Artie Shaw on the clarinet (earlier Sabrina had vetoed a rather puckish request for Sid Vicious and the Sex Pistols). She was speaking of poetry's place in the world of art when I told her what I believed *true* poetry to be.

"Poetry…is like my hand tracing the curve of your foot, moving slowly up your rounded calves to your luscious thigh where I pause for a taste of your essence before creeping to your mid-drift, savoring all your velvety texture, continuing to your breasts, resting on their softness, then running my tongue up the firm flesh of your neck-chin-lips, gently moving you to ecstasy."

Okay, it was corny, but what did I care? After all, I was a guy just wanting to get laid.

In bed, our world was bliss, but outside the bedroom we were sometimes querulous over different things, but we finally just got used to each other. Maybe we both got off on the heated arguments because they always ended up with a wild romp in the sack. But her friends— her 'coffeehouse commissar coterie' as I once angrily called them— had begun to wear thin on me. Before I went to the lake, the situation had become deleterious: Sabrina unconsciously threw their boilerplate jargon at me when we had personal disagreements; worse still, their general disdain and mendacity concerning all those they deemed 'privileged' rubbed off on her, causing Sabrina to sometimes misconstrue things I said and did.

I got tired of it all, though I often responded to her badly and am partially to blame. So, I took off to be alone. In fact, before Michael's visit, I had been toying with the idea of death.

I often wonder why fate throws people together when all they do is make each other nuts. What good does it do either when nights between sheets only lead to distance on the sofa? So many relationships, based on sex, produce marriages of regret. Some people foolishly try to salvage the wrecked relationship to no avail, often hurting the innocent products of their nighttime pleasures. Most drift apart from each other, living separate lives of twisted truths. Sabrina was never what many call a football widow, but neither was she a true soulmate. I felt like an FM transmitter trying to get through on an AM receiver. Sex brought us together, but love tore us apart.

Or was it fear?

As I listened to Michael's and Robyn's stories, I began to see my relationship with Sabrina for what it was, is, and could be. Instead of trying to assign blame, I should have been seeking understanding. We'd taken separate forks in the road we traveled together, that now seemed to be bending back towards the same path. But more than that, I felt Michael and Robyn, all the while, were trying to tell me something, the meaning of which remained just out of reach.

While I was working late one night, there came a timid knocking at the door. At first, I didn't pay it any mind, thinking it was only the house settling, or a limb rasping against a windowpane. Then the knocking sounded again, much louder. I stopped typing and cocked my ears to listen. Three distinct tap-tap-taps sounded on the wood. I had just started to rise from my chair when the door opened a crack and a pink face looked in.

"Excuse me, but I think I may be lost."

"Well," I said a little hoarsely, "if Michael or Robyn sent you, then you're at the right place."

"Oh…good, good." The man entered. He was dressed all in red (or it might have been burgundy) and his pinkish skin and eyes seemed alive with fever. In his trembling hands, he carried three leather bound books.

Running a sweaty hand through his coppery hair he sighed, "Would it be possible to get a tall glass of ice water? I fear my journey has exhausted me."

I directed him to the recliner, but he shied away from it taking a seat on the sofa instead. He laid the books on the coffee table as I handed him a glass filled with ice and water. When he touched the glass, I thought I heard a low sizzling and the ice seemed to rapidly melt away before the glass touched his lips. However, to be quite honest, it was a rather warm mid-summer night. Albeit, warmer than was usual.

"Thanks. Would it be a bother to ask for more? Perhaps a tall pitcher of ice?"

I brought out a pitcher of ice and water, mostly ice, and set it on the table. He took several pieces and rubbed them on his face.

"Ahhhhh...pure hea...heeeea...heaven." He looked at me with those red eyes swimming with moisture. "Thank you. You're a saaaa...saaaa...saint." I thought I saw him wince in pain.

"Not a problem." I replied, raising an eyebrow in fascination as he devoured several pieces of ice.

I picked up one of the books. "So, these are the diaries Michael promised to send?"

"Yes, yes. Our diaries. I'm sure they'll shed light on what your friends have left in shadow." The man drank the water from the pitcher with what seemed to be an unquenchable thirst. "Ahhhhh, *nothing* is as good as ice...cold...water."

"Would you like something to eat? I often have dinner about now."

"No, thank you. Just the water...and more ice, please. My time here is short."

I opened two of the books. Compared Michael's impatient scrawl to Robyn's delicate script. The words took me deeper into their ethereal world.

"They're one you know."

"What?" The man's words snapped me out of my trance.

"Your friends. They share one soul."

"I've noticed. It's rare for one to find their true soul mate."

"No...no. You don't understand at all. But how could you? Or any of us." He lowered his eyes, sighing heavily. "We're so easily led...." But he stopped in mid-sentence as if he had said too much.

I looked into the man's eyes. Into red watery swirls of light and dark. He touched my forearm. I jerked away in pain.

"But soon you *will* know all."

162

FINAL PHASE

UNEARTHLY POWERS

CHAPTER SEVENTEEN

July 2, 1985

A DARKNESS has swept over my soul like a thunder cloud hovering overhead, blocking out the stars and obscuring my vision. Since leaving Noble, Indiana—that quaint little hick town where sad-faced people live out their mundane lives blissfully ignorant of so many truths hidden in shadows—I have wandered the globe in search of some*thing* that will help me open the portal to true knowledge. Sometimes, I can sense that I am close to uncovering hidden knowledge only to have it slip away as a dream slips from the waking mind. It sometimes feels as if I am living in a perpetual state of déjà vu: doomed to relive the present life over and over until some last *key* is found to set me free upon a new destiny, yet unable to *see* the future clearly enough to find it. Almost as if I am living in a familiar, yet, shadowy world. Lost. Indeed, I feel that I am meant for something more than merely existing in this material world so bent upon self-destruction. My friend, the writer, whom Jase and I always thought to be a tad peculiar, would say that I am obsessed with the occult and have a death wish, or that I am attempting to run away from what truly scares me, living a long life without my soul mate, my one true love, Caryn. Perhaps he is correct on all accounts.

Her face I see everywhere. Sometimes, I see her in my dreams, and wake in the middle of the night, sweating and screaming out her name to the emptiness of my bedchamber, reaching out to a ghostly image mere inches from my grasp that slowly fades away. There are often others who appear in my dreams as well. A dark man completely hidden in shadow who taunts me; a tall blonde woman with swirling blue eyes, whom I must protect, but whom also I love. But our encounters are often cut short by such an oppressive presence of evil that I feel it is Lucifer himself who wants to keep us apart. For what reason, I cannot discover. Upon waking, I remind myself that these are only dreams, fantasies of a weary mind lost in a loveless world. Without her, all else is meaningless. Why then do I hold on so dearly to the tenets of truth and hope?

My soul was torn asunder the day Caryn died, torn apart by a freight train that seemed to appear from out of the fog like a behemoth rising up out of a darkened sea. I swore to never love another, and I have been true to my oath.

And so I wander aimlessly through life hoping beyond hope that I might quickly find death in order to relieve this heart-wrenching suffering of my soul. Lost. Alone. Damned.

I have prayed for death, sought death, even attempted to do myself in on several occasions, but the results were always a failure. Every time I return from a mission—missions that most consider to be suicidal—I curse the Creator for not allowing me to die, or pray that while I lie sleeping that death should come for me. Yet, the next morning when my eyes open and I realize that I have been doomed to live yet another day, I swear in despair.

One such morning, as I stumbled through my apartment in the false-dawn light of summer, I decided to force the issue and tempt fate. Taking my Berretta 9mm automatic from its holster, I sat on the sofa in the living room. As I sat in the semi-gloom, my entire life rolled by my mind's eye in brilliant technicolor images full of life, sounds and smells so vivid that I actually felt their aromas. I placed a full clip of bullets in the chamber and slid it closed, snapping back the slide to insert the first round. I felt calm, at peace with myself and the world as I placed the barrel into my mouth and squeezed the trigger ever so gently.

Snap. I blinked.

Checking the pistol, I saw that the hammer had indeed closed, but the round had not gone off. I slid the slide again, injecting a new round into the chamber. Again, the bullet failed to fire.

I repeated this action seven times with the same results. All the bullets were in pristine condition, so I reloaded the clip, pointed at a ceramic lamp, and fired. The pistol kicked, the lamp exploded, and smoke poured from the barrel. Again, I put the barrel in my mouth.

Snap. I reloaded the same bullet, aimed at the television, fired, and watched the set explode into dozens of pieces. I repeated this cycle for the next five bullets with the same results. In exasperation, I tossed the gun aside and laughed hysterically until the police arrived to question me about gunshot reports.

In my time, I have been shot, stabbed, poisoned, beaten, tossed out of planes and off of buildings, only to survive by some freak occurrence that miraculously saved me at the last possible second. My friends, back in Noble, always said I was golden-five-leaf-clover lucky, but I believe what happens to me has nothing to do with luck. It is something more insidious.

It sometimes feels as if death rides on my shoulder like a dark guardian ensuring that I come to no serious harm. When I aim to kill, the bullet finds its mark with ease; however, I seem to be immune from fatal injuries.

Perhaps I *am* merely ultra-lucky as my friends say. Perhaps. I will keep searching for the *key*, I suppose, because I know, more than just an itching at the back of one's mind, that I will find it one day. Or perhaps, if I am truly lucky, my luck will run out and I will rejoin Caryn beyond this veil.

CHAPTER EIGHTEEN

RoChelle

Halloween 1967

I was at my cabin by Kentucky Lake in Tennessee in 1997 trying to write and get my relationship with my wife straight in my head when a diary from my old childhood friend, Michael, arrived by special courier. As I sat in the glare of a single light, reading through his adventures, I came across an entry about a time in our youth that I had long forgotten.

From the Diary of Michael J. Bear

SOMETIMES, friends keep secrets from each other. You and Jase, I am sure, both kept secrets from me. There are just some things that are so personal we cannot help but want to keep them to ourselves. Although Jase was with me for the beginning of this story, I never told him, or anyone else, what happened to me later. Hopefully, when you read this, my good friend, you will forgive me, my selfishness, and understand my reasons for remaining silent all these years.

It all began Halloween night in 1967. Jase and I had been out most of the night soaping windows and rolling yards like many teenagers did back then. Just good harmless fun. It was nearing ten o'clock when we found ourselves on Main Street passing by the Nelson Estate. You remember, the estate where that elderly woman lived who we all thought was a witch. Well, as we walked along the sidewalk, thankfully hidden from sight by the tall shrubberies, we heard a lot of racket coming from the mansion.

"What the heck you think they're doing up in there tonight?" Jase said, and I thought, a little nervously.

"How should I know?" I may have sounded harsher than I should have, but Jase didn't seem to notice.

"Cause your family is part of that society, that's why."

It's funny how people with money are always thought of as being a part of an intimate club by people with almost no money, but to tell the truth, there are degrees, and then there are secret corridors, within so-called 'high society.' Besides, Old Missus Nelson belonged to that level that had no dealings what-so-ever with small timers like my parents. And as far as I knew, Missus Nelson never had dealings with anyone in Noble, being what people call a recluse.

"Jase, just because somebody has money, doesn't mean they get invitations to parties given by people like Missus Nelson. She belongs to the elite. I doubt anyone in Noble is wealthy enough to receive invitations to her parties." Naturally, this made Jase scratch his head. Remember how he used to do that every time he encountered something he could not comprehend? Jase would get this highly confused look on his face, and scratch his head.

Anyway, after a moment he says, "Let's git a peek up in thar," reverting to his thick eastern Kentucky accent.

Heck, it was early, so I figured, why not have some real excitement for a change? Man, I wish you had been there. Maybe…but that is the past after all, is it not? We are both older now and, after everything we have encountered over the years, wise enough to admit things we could not in our youth.

You know, I never could understand why, if old Missus Nelson had so much money, she never built a wall up around her property. There were just those eight-foot-high bushes that ran along the sidewalk on Main Street, down Center Street, and around the far side and back of the house. As we made our way through one of the little tunneled openings in the bushes, I thought about the castle where Sleeping Beauty lived surrounded by her thorn bushes, and wondered if Missus Nelson had some young maiden held captive in that spiral tower on the north side of the mansion.

"Sure is a lot of commotion going on. Must be sum big ole party tonight," Jase said, as we lay on the Bermuda grass just beyond the bush line. "Look at all them cars." He whistled low.

"Dang," I whispered, "you notice anything weird about those cars?"

"Nawp." Then he spat and said, "Unless you're talkin' 'bout how they're all black."

"Yeah. Don't you think that's a bit odd? I mean, every guest arriving in a black car?" I was beginning to get one of those spooky feelings you're always going on about.

"Don' rightly know, bud." Jase was watching with fascination as the line of black cars cycled up the paved driveway as they were guided to parking slots in the yard.

I figured if a good rain sprung up, that Missus Nelson would have one heck of a messy yard come morning. But the night, as you will remember, was clear. So clear, in fact, that we could see nothing but stars, and that big ole full Moon, hanging right over the top of Missus Nelson's mansion. Or so it seemed.

We stayed there for a long time watching men and women, all dressed in fancy black evening attire, some with capes, exit their cars and stroll up those big stone steps into the mansion. Classical music, Bach, or maybe Wagner, played so loud we could hear it even as far away as we were and there were so many screams and other forms of revelry going on that, in all truth, I felt my hair standing on end. God, I thought I even heard the howl of a couple of wolves.

"Dang! Did you hear that Jase?" I looked over at him. He'd heard. I knew, because his face was white and his eyes looked like they were about to pop out of his head.

"Holy mother in heaven, Michael! What in the world was that?"

"A wolf, I think."

"Maybe it's just a recording playing?" He ventured hopefully, speaking more plainly.

"Maybe." You remember how some people would play those records of spooky sounds at Halloween parties? Well, once we started rationalizing and all, we relaxed a bit. "Yeah. Has to be a recording."

"Yeah."

Then this man, he must have been six foot or better, walks out onto the veranda into the light and I see he has the whitest face I've ever seen up to that point. His hair was long and black, and his eyes looked red. I say this because, I swear, they glowed! He was dressed in a fancy black tuxedo and cape and carried a black walking stick. Well, he stands there for a bit, scanning the yard as if he is looking for something. I figured there wasn't much he could see with all those cars and the big old oak and willow trees scattered about with their branches swaying in a breeze that suddenly sprung up.

I looked over at Jase and he was shaking like a leaf in a tornado.

"Look at him, Jase. Now, he is spooky." I whispered, but just barely.

"I think he heard you, man." Jase was scooting backwards into the bushes.

I didn't, at the time, know how he could have; however, he did look in our direction and frown. Then this short woman with bushy brown hair wearing a black dress with what looked like silver threads in the form of what I took to be a spider's web comes out a side door. She starts speaking to him, pulling at his arm in a way that suggested, to me, she wanted him to go back inside the house.

As the man complied, the woman turned towards me and winked. Jase about lost it then.

"Wha' the heck was that?" He asked from inside the bushes.

"It was probably just a trick of the light." But I wondered.

After a while, people started coming out and getting into their cars, so I scooted back up inside the bushes with Jase. We watched as the cars, one by one, drove away. When all the guests had departed, I saw all the lights in the mansion start going out, room by room, until only one light up in that tower room was left burning.

Jase started getting his nerve back and dared me to go up and ring the doorbell.

"Why don't you do it?" I snapped.

"Heck, Michael, what's wrong? No courage?" I thought he was one to talk after the way he'd been shaking most of the night.

"Me? Nothing scares me. I just think if you want to play a trick then you should be the one to do it." I was scared, but was not about to admit that to Jase.

"You run faster than I do," he said, urging me on by stroking my ego.

Now you know as well as I do that Jase was just about the fastest sprinter in our school, besides Sean MacIonorrie. I figured he was just itching to see if I would do it or not. So, I stood up and said, "Fine. If you're such a chicken, I'll do it." I trotted off towards the nearest oak.

The run from the front door to the bushes I gauged to be around 40 or 50 yards. Five seconds, or so, I figured it would take to close the distance, if my feet didn't betray me and send me tumbling to the ground or smacking into a tree.

Slowly, I made my way from tree to tree until I reached the circular driveway in front of the house. There was this big fountain with three marble angels in the center pouring water and I ran to it, hunching down below the rim. The garden statues were surrounded by rose shrubs that, despite the mid-autumn season, seemed in full bloom. These were the most beautiful roses I had ever seen because they emanated red and golden glows of light. (I think 'rutilant' would be your word.) It reminded me of something from a Beauty and the Beast fairytale.

Peeking around, I saw that everything was still quiet—no people, no sounds and no lights. So I ran and sailed up the steps to the porch. I was breathing heavily, nervous as heck, and sweating. But I gathered my courage and reached out to ring the doorbell.

That's when the heavy oaken French doors flew open and someone grabbed me by the arm!

Jase must have yelled in fright because I heard a high-pitched scream followed by what sounded like feet beating the pavement of the sidewalk out by the bushes. The night was so quiet his feet sounded like sledgehammers hitting cement.

I tried to pull away from who, or whatever, had grabbed me, but their grip was like a steel bear trap around my bicep.

"What do we have here? Rats come nibbling at my door?" Before I could blink, I was pulled inside and the big doors slammed shut behind me.

You pretty much knew the story up to this point. What happened next is what I have kept secret for all these years. I felt it necessary to refresh your memory, just in case you had forgotten.

Once inside, whoever had a hold of me shut the doors and threw on the light in the foyer. I was so busy struggling and trying to get free that I didn't pay attention to anything else. Then I heard a voice, like clear water coursing down a brook, say, "Relax. You're not in any trouble."

I stopped fighting and looked at my captor. She was beautiful, the kind of woman who inspired the phrase 'drop-dead gorgeous.' I found myself looking into the eyes of a girl not much older than we were then, with long blonde/white hair that hung in twisting curls down to her waist. But her eyes were even more amazing! Not only were they beautiful, they really did sparkle. They were large, round and bluer than any blue I have ever seen. She let me go and crossed her arms, giving me a look I took to be either approval or annoyance. It was hard to say because of those mystical eyes, and the tiny smile dancing across her full, come-give-me-a-kiss lips.

I was completely mesmerized by her stare that didn't waver. She didn't even blink. She just stood there looking at me, and waiting. Well, I was getting fairly nervous after a couple of minutes, so I finally said, "Look, we only meant to play a harmless prank. You know how it is, being Halloween and all."

Her smile widened and she nodded. "Oh yes. Tonight is All Hallows Evening, isn't it?"

She ran her short brown fingers through her hair and let out a laugh that kind of thrilled but scared me all at the same time. Her nails were long and pointed, and painted with a high gloss black polish that reflected the modest light from the lamps.

"Well, I suppose such pranks on this special night should be expected. However," she moved her head ever so slightly so I could see her nice firm neck with smooth brown skin, "no one has been brave enough to disturb my solitude before. Especially during the time of Hallowtide."

I swallowed hard, part in fear, part in a rising pressure that was throbbing in my jeans, and part in wonder. My eyes just could not stop taking in her beauty. She was my height and slim, and the black dress she wore was mid-length and had a low-cut front that gave me a really good view of her smooth round cleavage. She also was wearing a black choker studded with diamonds that enhanced her natural beauty. The longer I stood there looking at her, the more nervous I became. And you know I don't really get nervous around girls. She must have sensed my feelings because she smiled and laughed again.

"Perhaps we should go into the parlor where you might be more comfortable."

I think my leg was shaking like yours was that night we had dinner with Caitlyn. She turned, ever so slightly, and seemed to actually float through an archway into the parlor where a fire was crackling away in the fireplace. As she passed me, a bit close I might add, I smelled the sweet scent of peonies on her. Watching her walk with her back to me, her slim hips swaying evenly, made my leg twitch more as I hobbled after her.

"Sit, please."

She was sitting on a black velvet divan with her legs crossed, as she indicated a big over-stuffed black leather chair. Wow, she had really nice legs. Slim, athletic and well-toned. I could see they were bare because they were the same shade of light brown as her face and hands, and were smooth, and I thought must feel like satin. On her feet were black patent leather pumps with three-inch heels that had rubies on the buckles. I made an adjustment as I sat, feeling my face turn red.

"Tea?" She asked, as I sat uneasily on the edge of the cushions.

"Umm, sure."

She leaned over and poured me a cup of tea from a silver teakettle that was sitting on the coffee table. The black china cup and saucer she handed me were delicate, and I knew that the entire set must have cost a fortune—a lot more expensive than anything my parents had—which didn't make me feel any more relaxed because I was afraid I would drop and break them. The tea was sweet and hot, with just the hint of a spice I could not identify. As I drank, it coursed through my body making me feel a little tingly.

There wasn't much light in the room, but I could see that it was decorated in an Old Gothic style. In addition, there were suits of armor, weapons of all kinds—swords, axes, lances, maces, shields— from Roman to Medieval European, and Asian bamboo armor from the Ming Dynasty. I knew about such things because I read so much about ancient weaponry and such. The walls were covered with paintings by Van Gogh, da Vinci, Lippi, Dali and several by Rossetti. However, all the themes in the paintings were Gothic in nature, which I thought was a bit strange. There was even a huge German tapestry depicting the hunt and slaughter of, all things, vampires. And one, especially disturbing painting, depicting a beautiful gypsy being ravished by an extremely menacing werewolf. In all truth, I half expected to see a coffin, but didn't.

"How do you like my collection?" She said casually as I gazed around. "Most of the items are rare and one of a kind. As I'm sure you've noticed."

She was beginning to get spookier. I had the idea she could read my mind, then thought, *heck, most people in town know about my research concerning the occult and ancient philosophies, and my perfect memory. Why wouldn't the elite gentry?* I figured she probably knew who I was and was pulling my leg about the house being hers, probably to teach me a lesson about respecting one's privacy by trying to give me a good scare. Heck, I knew there was no way she could be Missus Nelson.

Then she tilted her head back and laughed, and I shivered. She had shiny white teeth that were perfectly even except for the canines that I thought were a tad long. Every second I gazed at her, I saw more details that really made my blood pump. I was torn between fear and excitement. So I drank more tea hoping it would relax me a little more. The tea cup vibrated on the saucer as I set it back down.

"Now," she bit her bottom lip and studied me critically with those ever-shifting swirls of blue enhanced by black eyeliner and the lightest of blue eye shadow, "what am I to do with you? Hmmm."

I choked on the tea. *Holy cow*, I thought, *she is a witch, or a vampire, and is going to eat me.* Naturally, about as soon as that thought raced through my mind, I knew it wasn't true. She just looked far too young to be Missus Nelson, *but*, I reminded myself, *she did call it her house.* It was about that time that my nervousness abated and I entered my serious mode. *Bunk*, I thought, *there are no such things as witches, vampires or werewolves. She is just paying me back with a prank of her own, trying to make me think she's Missus Nelson. She's probably some relative or visitor. Those teeth are probably porcelain; she certainly has enough money, whoever she is, to afford such elaborate props.*

"Umm, I did apologize, ma'am, and you did say earlier that I wasn't in any trouble." I tried to make an appeal to reason, hoping she wouldn't call my parents.

"RoChelle, please, and yes, I did say that, but I just can't decide." She was eyeing me pretty closely, so I grabbed my heart and stuffed it back into my chest.

"Decide?" I asked, raising an eyebrow.

"Yeees," she drew out her vowels and consonants like Caitlyn used to when she wanted to emphasize something, "whether or not you're…worthy."

You remember how it was when you were 16 and making out with a pretty girl, and you just knew by the way she kissed and moved that you were about to get laid? That's how I felt.

Sighing, she stood up, and wiggled her fingers at me. "Come with me please."

I gulped. When I took hold of her hand, a warm excited feeling rushed through my body. Her hand was soft, and cool, but strong. We laced our fingers together and proceeded out of the parlor, down the front hall to a stairway I just knew had to lead to that tower room.

We walked up a dark spiral staircase that emptied out into a circular room painted black. The only pieces of furniture were two bedside nightstands—one had a vase mixed with peonies and roses; the other a large wooden box with a round top—and a huge black walnut canopy bed with black sheets and several large pillows in black cases. The light came from a giant chandelier made of silver in the design of a pentagram. There were holders on each star point containing long black candles, slowly burning. As I walked into the room, I smelled the thick aroma of cinnamon.

RoChelle opened the box on the opposite nightstand, put on some white gloves, and began slowly assembling pins, needles, and a bracket with an arm of sorts. She pulled a large brass horn from nowhere, and I realized RoChelle was assembling an old phonograph machine, perhaps an Edison antique. She began winding the bracket, then picked up a black tube and fitted it onto a shiny cylinder. Once she'd finished, she turned her gaze at me. RoChelle removed her white gloves, turned down the sheets, stood before me and smiled. I was in awe and stunned as she slipped out of her shoes, dropped her dress to her ankles, and slowly stepped out of it. A more exquisite female form I had never, and never have since, seen. It was all I could do to contain myself. (Just so you know, in a situation like that, reciting mathematical equations in your head helps.)

The phonograph began to play, but, instead of some 1890s lilting tune, the voice was from The Platters' 1958 classic, "Smoke Gets in Your Eyes." The music rolled forth clearly with no hint of lossy scratchiness or vinyl distortion: the sound was clearer than a compact disc. The wistful song, the 19th century phonograph, the dark room, the enchanting girl—none of it made sense, but all was real.

RoChelle slipped beneath the sheets and motioned for me to join her. I'll spare you the details, but the sun was about to rise by the time we'd finished.

"Okay, it is time for you to leave."

She kissed me, ever so delicately, and walked me to the door.

"One night," she said, opening the door for me, "is all I can give you. But, I trust it has been one you'll remember."

She had that right.

Naturally, I wasn't going to let her get away so easily, so for several days after that night I went by the estate hoping to get a glimpse of her, but I never did. The only person I did see was old Missus Nelson out working in the yard with the roses or walking along the veranda, her long white hair hanging down in waves past her waist.

I figured that RoChelle must have been a relative or something, and had only been visiting, so I gave up looking for her. But one day in April, when I was passing by, Missus Nelson was near the front entrance planting some peonies and roses by the side of the drive. Her hair was rolled up under this big wide-brimmed straw hat and she was wearing a black dress that revealed enough to show me that she really wasn't as old as we'd all thought. I figured she was around 40 or so, because her face was rather smooth and brown. Truthfully, she probably could have passed for a woman in her late twenties.

As I walked past, eyeing her with curiosity, she looked me, and I thought I saw her blue eyes sparkling as she winked.

NOTE

First published in Mallorn *54 in the Spring 2013 volume. (Courtesy of the Tolkien Society, UK)*

EPILOGUE

Summer's End 1997

MICHAEL told stories of living, Robyn of the dead, and Cain of fate. Perhaps they were trying to tell me about myself; the terrible mistake I could avoid if only I would listen.

I spent several days reading over the manuscripts after transcribing their stories. Their words echoed through my soul and renewed my spirit. I was listening to vintage music from 1968 when I finished my first edit of the transcripts. The oldies station was playing "The Porpoise Song" as I turned and looked in the direction of the lake. Sabrina loves the ocean; I haven't anything against it: the sounds of waved winds moving through sea oats and palm trees, together with twin sunsets on water, is enchanting. That said, I prefer the tranquility of lakes: gentle waters broach the shoreline, loud enough to calm the soul, but the volume never blots out birdsong or cicada. I often enjoy sunsets or early morning sunrises while deer or small animals enter the yard and eye me with curiosity.

The Monkees finished their song about the "clock in the sky," and I decided to take a break before starting another edit. As I walked through the woods, I tried to comprehend Gaia's purpose. Tonight, I saw misty images of Michael dancing across the lakeshore like funny old Bojangles, or waltzing with Robyn, both wearing white and black evening attire, like Astaire and Rogers, the moonlight bathing them in its spotlight, the lunar glow sparkling off their twin silver triquetra pendants.

Summer was coming to an end. I wondered if Sabrina would be home, waiting for me. She would undoubtedly bombard me with questions about what I'd been writing all summer. I also thought about the New Age philosophy students who always, while telling beer-sodden lies at Foucault's Tavern, questioned the value of their degrees.

People say in these days that there is too much being written. That there cannot be anything new when nothing is new. But is that right? No. Yes. Maybe. No one can truly know for sure.

Maybe, who knows, there will come a time when mankind will evolve from its present selfishness into something akin to godhead: more like, a restored humanity that comes from a renewed and unbroken connection to the cosmic and divine. If the source of that connection is a triune God, so be it.

But that is of little concern to me at present.

After all, nothing really matters but love. Through love, we learn to live our lives better. And living life to the fullest is of greater importance than trying to make sense of it. Surely, if there is a Creator—yes, I now believe there is one—then there has to be more to existence than what we know. But how much do we really need to know? Perhaps only that two can make one.

Fate and predestination are meaningless when it comes to our daily bread. We can only accept what comes our way and shape our own worlds accordingly. Like God, we are subcreators who can forge (if not escape, at least alone) our own heavens and hells. But unlike God, we must struggle with the darker side of ourselves to see the light. At all moments and beyond, the world likewise is full of darkness and light that contends with us.

Everything is summed up by saying it is all a matter of faith, and we are told that those without faith are lost.

It is not that simple.

I know Sabrina will be waiting for me at our home. Is that faith? Perhaps. Maybe it's nothing more than a fool's hope. Maybe her return from California will be delayed…indefinitely. No, these are foolish questions, foolish worries. She will be there. I know now what drove us apart. It was my own twisted sense of reality. She was not the lost soul searching for a guide. It was I who feared the shadows dancing on the wall. And fearing insanity would take hold of my soul, I fled into the woods, into my own wilderness, to seek something I could not identify.

Sabrina is the rock, the foundation on which our love will grow into a spiritual merging. We have always been one, and always will be one, soul. The telephone sits on the coffee table; my half-full brandy glass sits beside it. I have passed through the black hole of doubt and emerged a new person. I dial our number but replace the receiver before the second ring ends. Lying back on the sofa, I close my eyes. My body relaxes and I feel a new lightness come over me. I can hear Benny Goodman playing "The World is Waiting for the Sunrise." We no longer need technological intermediaries to connect us. I reach out with my mind, feeling at peace with life, and mentally caress hers.

Caitlyn...Jaid. Sabrina. I Believe.

To learn more of Michael, Robyn, and Cain, please read Professor Ridge's novel Between Shadows *(available through Author House).*

CONVERSATIONS

MICHALSKI: Let's start out with your childhood; where are you from and how did you grow up? How did this affect your decisions in life?

RIDGE: I grew up in a small farming community in central Indiana where I lived until 1976. Most of my youth was spent riding horses through the woods of southern Indiana with my friends and camping, hiking, and exploring adventures with the Boy Scouts and Explorers. I wrote my first short story at the age of twelve, having already spent many years reading biographies, adventure stories, and day-dreaming while riding alone in the woods. Throughout Junior High and High school, I wrote poetry and stories and began my first novel. Although I was an athlete and fair student, I spent most of my time alone, except for two good friends, one of which also owned horses. My frustrations with lower-middle-class life and not having anyone [teachers, parents, etc.] as supporters, I left home after graduation to join the Navy. That was November 1976 and I have never really returned home.

MICHALSKI: How did you become interested in your field? What brought you to writing and publishing? How did you get involved with online blogs and editing and publishing?

RIDGE: I have always written on my own. In Junior High I found an old hand-powered printing press and was allowed to experiment with this technology while the other students worked in mock-businesses. In 1992, I began learning the programming language for the Web and started creating web pages. There were a lot of online poetry sites in the early days of the web, so I started testing the waters there. I soon learned that most sites were questionable and would take anything submitted. I proved this by writing a nonsense poem backwards and upside down, which several sites accepted with praise. I have since then avoided online publications unless I know the editors or deem the site to be professionally made.

MICHALSKI: How did you begin writing your books? What all does it take to accomplish writing a book?

RIDGE: Sometimes stories develop over time, and sometimes they just come to the writer. Some writing instructors may have a lot to say on the so-called 'art and craft' of writing, but I don't. My novel began as a series of unrelated short stories that I transformed into a larger story. A few years after letting it sit on the shelf, I took it down and began reshaping the story and the way it unfolds. Writing a book takes patience and determination. Instead of worrying over the theme, or grammar, or characters, just write it all down, and save the cosmetic things for afterwards. Let the characters speak to you instead of trying to force events. If your short stories tend to run long, then maybe you are a novelist.

MICHALSKI: Are there any challenges to your field? Or any instances that you remember being particularly difficult?

RIDGE: Writing is a challenge every time you start anything new. Teaching is a daily challenge. The most difficult thing about my job is time management. Teaching classes, running a writing center—alone—taking on the administrative responsibilities of a department head, and dealing with student problems daily leaves very little time for personal writing, research, or relaxing.

MICHALSKI: Any advice or tips for an online blog editor?

RIDGE: Advice for an online blog editor? Just keep your writing focused on facts, and do not allow yourself to fall into the trap of writing emotionally-driven diatribes. Always give your readers the various viewpoints of any topic without placing judgments on any one side.

NOTE

Published originally in the Freedom's Hill Primer *on March 22, 2018.*

THE AUTHOR

A BRIEF NOTE

MARC RIDGE was born in central Indiana to one of the families that had migrated from rural Kentucky and settled there to farm and work. As a child, Ridge's upbringing was rich in friends, family, and experiences if not with money; some of his published stories delve into the lives of children who grow up in a fictionalized Midwestern town. The children in these stories (who are later teenagers) spend their formative years learning to overcome fears of personal isolation and unknown forces by embracing the values of acceptance, fellowship, and belief. Ridge always maintained that his childhood mirrored that of his characters.

Ridge's parents and older siblings encouraged him to be a voracious reader and to become a lifelong learner. This came natural to the creative boy who dove into the classics of the ancient world as well as literature and contemporary fiction. As a school student, Ridge also had an aptitude for science and math, and his teachers encouraged him to explore technology and problem-solving.

Though he excelled in his classes, Ridge's parents could not afford to send him to the local college. To earn money for his university education, Ridge enlisted in the U.S. Navy and made a career for himself in the service of his country. When Ridge shared his experiences of being a seaman and later an enlisted officer, he often had a conflicted opinion about his time in the military. On the one hand, he was proud of his service, and there were adventures to be had onboard an aircraft carrier; traveling to remote and exotic lands appealed to Ridge and provided materials for his personal studies and creative works. On the other hand, Ridge also conveyed that navy life and routine did not always suit his creative or intellectual sensibilities. Throughout his naval career, Ridge continued to harbor a deep love for words and stories, and he never lost sight of his goal to complete his college education.

While still on active duty, Ridge began to gravitate towards teaching as his vocation. He was asked to be an instructor to other servicemen (and servicewomen) who needed to learn the basics of aircraft maintenance. It was as a naval instructor that Ridge realized how he could combine his love for stories with his call to teach into a new career. From that moment on, Ridge prepared for his second career as a college English professor.

Ridge completed his degrees in English at the University of Memphis before enrolling into their creative writing program. After teaching at a couple of colleges and vocational institutions (including spending a couple of years as an instructor in China), Ridge came to Rust College to be the Writing Center Director. At Rust, Ridge was a fixture on the campus, and he eventually became the Coordinator for the English Department.